ON THE LAKEFRONT

XAVIER PHLICK

Cover Design: Swamynathan Arumugam from India

ISBN 978-1-7361164-0-1 (hardback)
ISBN 978-1-7361164-1-8 (paperback)
ISBN 978-1-7361164-2-5 (mobi)
ISBN 978-1-7361164-3-2 (epub)
ISBN 978-1-7361164-4-9 (audiobook)

ACKNOWLEDGMENTS

Thank you to everyone who supports me, whether it is family or any part of my social circles. I really could not have done it without your love and support. Thank you for supporting me through my ups and downs over the past year.

Dear God, thank you for giving me a story to tell. When I prayed for strength and understanding, you gave it to me. Our relationship is one I will never be able to explain or let go of.
Thank you a million times for my life.

PROLOGUE

OCTOBER 25, 2018

"This is Tom Sells and Veronica Edwards here at WLAS Channel 5 broadcast—the most viewed news in the New Orleans, Metairie, Kenner, and all other surrounding areas." The reporter had a professional tone.

"Real news events first."

"Tom," Veronica interrupts, "We are getting the breaking story of a body found in a car where there might be some foul play involved. Marcia Jones and our street team are on the scene. Marcia."

"Good evening, Veronica. I am located where a passerby called with a tip about a strange automobile. They said they went up to the car, noticed blood, and called authorities. This silver 2016 Toyota Camry behind me is where they discovered the body. The NOPD is processing this scene as a homicide. A gun and note found on the scene suggested it was suicide. Police say that the victim is an unidentified African-American male around the ages of 21 to 30. They will release more details, including the victim's identity, once police notify the family. I am Marcia Jones with WLAS Channel 5 news."

"Is this happening? Nah," the young man said. He clicked the TV off. "Is that why you haven't come? Bredda Weh a you?" He peered out his window, looking at the spot where his brother would park.

He said with a sigh to himself, "Well, I haven't gotten a call so." Just then, his cell phone interrupted his thoughts. "Yow madda Wah a wrong? Mi jus did si di news An...." He said in a whisper before becoming loud. "Yuh a lie. Dat a nah fi mi bredda. Mi haffi guh." He hung the phone up in disbelief, and the tears flowed.

MEANWHILE, at home in Kenner, a couple is sitting up in their bed. The husband just turned off the TV.

"My poor student," he said, making his way to the restroom with his phone in his hand.

"You bring your cell phone in the bathroom?" she asked, giving him a dirty look.

"Man, can I go take a shit and play candy crush in peace?"

She scoffed and rolled over as he went into the bathroom. He started playing candy crush, but all the while, he was texting.

Little Nut, the mission is complete. Thank you for helping me take care of my dilemma.

He received a text back. *No problem, man.*

The guy then deleted the messages, flushed the toilet, and cleaned up to make it seem like he used it. He crawled back into bed and cradled his wife.

"Sometimes hurt people hurt people," he said in a mumble in her ear, brushing back her dreadlocks with his fingers.

She felt a teardrop on her face. She sensed her husband knew more about the news story.

1

PACK IT UP

"Aiden Phillips," she called my name as I was packing my overnight suitcase, "I know you hear me talking to you."

By the time I finished packing, I had looked up. Joanne was standing at my open bedroom door. All of 5 feet 2 inches with a low salt and pepper afro, this lady stared at me with a puzzled look on her face.

"I know my child. He is not a morning person," she huffed. "So…"

"Uh, mama. You must have forgotten the Wayne concert is today." I gave an explanation. "Me and Danielle going to the concert. Even though it's later on tonight, I wanna go see her and my cousins and be at Momo Jean's house."

I peeked into her eyes, and I figured what was next. I reached for her and embraced her, crying with her. During that embrace, I thought of everything that little lady meant to me.

JEAN PIERRE PHILLIPS, or Momo Jean, had died on August 24, five days before the 14th anniversary of Hurricane Katrina. At 88, she passed in her sleep. Momo was an exceptional mother to her four children, Joanne, my mom & her oldest, John, David, Jr., and her deceased son, Connor. Of course, she was a wonderful grandmother to her eight grandchildren, Regina, David the III, Melissa, Jacob, Terrence, Jackson, Danielle, and me. She had loved us all equally, but the closest ones to her were my mommy and me. We embodied her giving spirit and family values; also, we exhibited her kindness, strength, and other ways. The only time she became frantic with my parent was when mom stayed in Marais Vert, a suburban area town 45 minutes away from Downtown Baton Rouge. Momo Jean preferred to move back home, but mom did not. However, her frustrations were short-lived as she welcomed that 2-hour drive to come and stay with us sometimes. It was especially true when one of her other kids got on her nerves or when she wished for a quieter scene.

She was no longer on this earth. Her burial was as grand as her heart was. Everyone said their goodbyes at the beginning of the function. The end of the service did not include a final viewing. It would be hard for the family to handle. Mom and I were the last people to view her. I was told by the funeral director how to tuck in my beloved Momo Jean. Then my mother and I gazed at her peacefully rested face and closed the casket together. The choir went through a musical barrage of contemporary gospel and old negro spirituals. Pastor Fredrick McKee, the Pastor of Agape Faith, eulogized her with tremendous personal antidotes and positive remarks on how she dedicated her life to God, family, and friends. The pallbearers moved in front of the casket while we were heading out. That is when our sentiments took hold of us. I hugged mom then like I was hugging her now. We relived that moment that changed our lives.

"I'M SORRY, son. I notice this is the first time you are traveling to the city since mama's death. How will you handle being at the house?" she asked. She realized she would set off some concerns.

"Well, mommy, Danielle is meeting me up there. She knows, and you are aware I am a terrible driver," I state as my mom's laugh comes flying. "Jackson and Terrence will be there. More than likely, Jacob will appear. So we all be at the house."

"How will you take it if Jim and Melissa arrive and visit?" she asked with concern, "I don't need to run down there, huh?"

"Mommy, I put it behind me. He knows what he did. Pretty sure she realizes it too. He will always be a creep I try to ignore," I stated with remorse. I didn't want my thoughts to be about them. My mom nor I spoke to him, but we embraced my cousin. After all, she was family no matter what happened in the past.

"Ok, just be careful and here," she said as she tossed me an orange medicine bottle, "make sure you pack these."

"Thanks, ma," I said as I placed them in my bag. I guess I was ready to face my emotions and fears.

2

PRE-CHILL AT MOMO JEAN'S

I tossed my bag into my 2015 gray Chevy Sonic. My to-do list gets checked before I leave home. I went through my phone for notices and playlist options. But I had two notifications on my iPhone. One was a text from Danielle saying that she cannot wait to see me and spend time with me.

However, the following notification puzzled me. It appeared from the app: HBG. I had not checked "Hot Black Guys" in a while, so I reviewed my one new message.

I want to meet you.

The profile stats seemed just my type: 6 feet 2 inches, African-American, and 24 years old. It sounded like a pretty good catch to me. The only problem I had was no profile picture. A blank profile with words most of the time, to me, means catfish. So, I just ignored it and started scrolling on what playlist to put on.

I have always had an eclectic taste in music. I have music from the Beatles, Otis Redding, Tina Turner, Aretha Franklin, Elvis Presley to Shawn Mendes, Beyoncé, Corinne Bailey Rae, and my favorite, Nicki Minaj. Lyrics and beats move me no matter what artist or genre. I was going through my playlist, and all the genres were popping up: Country, Reggae, Reggaeton, 90s pop, 00s pop, New Orleans bounce, Slow Jams, Rap, Hip Hop, Techno, EDM, and so on. After searching for that long time, I finally found my Weezyana Concert playlist, which comprised my favorite songs by artists performing in the lineup. I just knew I was about to jam to Wayne, Meek Mill, Trey Songz, and one of my new favorites, Megan the Stallion. Finally pressing play, I started driving, and let the music shuffle for the whole 2-hour drive. I pulled up to Momo Jean's house at 11 AM on the dot. That's when "Hot Girl Summer" came through the speakers. I was rapping it, looking in my mirror. A figure ran off the porch unseen by me. It went to the car door and knocked on my window. I was so startled that I cut the music down. I rolled down the window, and I had to stare. Danielle, my Uncle David's daughter, was giving me a dirty look, staring back at me.

"Cousin, if you don't get out of this car," she stated as the sun hit her beautiful creole skin and sandy golden hair. I got out of the car and hugged my cousin. She had been there for me during this entire ordeal. "Oh, my God.

Cousin, I know we all needed some time. Damn Cousin, I thought we would have been in more of contact."

"Yeah, Cuz. I'm sorry I have just been sticking to myself," I paused, "It really has been hard for me. I am still processing it. We will survive this as a family."

"All of us," she smirked, "including Melissa and her creep of a husband? When she brought him around, he would look at all of us. Especially you, though. I mean, he would stare at you for the longest time and..."

"Melissa," I said to my cousin, "will always be family. Now, as far as her husband goes. I definitely do not want to talk about how he..."

"Say Cuz," a familiar voice butted in, "You ain't text me. Let me call Tee Joanne to let her know you are here. You know she is worrisome."

I looked up, and it was Jackson, my favorite male cousin. The color of an oatmeal cookie & standing at 5 feet 9 inches, he was the male cousin I admired the most. He was the one that didn't judge me for being myself. He was my little protector.

"My bad, Cuz. We coming," I said. I followed Danielle up the stairs and onto the porch. She opened the door, and we walked inside. That was the moment I saw her. I was standing there in a trance directly in front of a beautiful 11 X 17 portrait of Momo Jean. She was smiling at me, bright as the sun, in her all-white ushers' uniform. As tears rolled down my face, I slid on the couch to catch myself.

"Man, bruh, I know it is tough, but stay strong." A deep voice had entered the room. This dark-skinned 6 feet 6 inches, 295-pound man, Terrence, Jackson's brother, was that voice. He is my big protector. "If you need that smoke, you know I got you."

"Thanks, Cuz. But, you know I don't smoke," I said.

"Right, Right," he said with a smirk. "Well, let me call one of my hoes. You gotta get some pussy. Cuz mane look, I'm tellin' you, if you can't hit the weed, at least hit that."

"Terrence!" I said in a scream and laugh. I could barely get words out of my mouth. "Cousin, leave me alone. I don't want no pussy cat, no Egyptian Mau, no Tom & Jerry, no Puss in Boots, no Catwoman, sidebar, although Eartha Kitt, Halle Berry, and Michelle Pfeiffer were all great. This guy doesn't like cats. At all. Period."

Jackson and Danielle came out of the kitchen with Zapp's salt & vinegar bags bursting out in laughter.

"Bro, push over Big T," Jackson said, still snickering as they sat between us, "and if you got any smoke, go roll it, and I'll smoke wit you. Please don't call your hoes, though, because I saw one of them. I wouldn't want cat from them either."

"Shut up, dawg. I got some pretty ones, but I keep them where they at. Hoes can come to the house. The ones that say yes. I can tell they ain't ya type," he huffed.

"Yeah, I don't want those chicken-head girls you be messing wit. Man, did this couch breathe?" Jack exhaled. Terrence playfully hit him in the arm as he went to the back. "Ouch!"

"Man, some things never change." I said in a mumble; turning to Dani, I asked, "So girlie, what time are we leaving? You know that parking is hell. Especially when we travel down in all that traffic."

"Well, it's only 10:30. We will leave at 11:15 since the parking opens at 12," Dani responded.

"Girl, you know how the traffic is. I gotta be the first one in line. Plus, they moved to the grounds from last year. We don't want to lose the spots we always have."

"Ok, Cousin, seeing as you dressed and you are making sense, I guess we can leave now."

"Man, you didn't want to hang with your cousin anymore, huh?" Jack said in a quiet tone.

"Cousin, I love you. But we will hang tomorrow. It will piss me off if I ain't front and center," I pouted.

"Cool, y'all, be safe. I guess I smoke wit my big bro or study."

Dani had gone into the guest room. She returned with her purse and everything she needed.

"You ready, Aiden?" she asked.

"Yep!" I said as I raced out the door to her car. "Bye, Jack. Remember, a promise is a promise."

Jackson nodded his head as he stood at the door. Dani was already walking to her blue 2017 Ford Focus. She pressed the button, and we both hopped in. We were on our way to our favorite event.

3

REVEALS, CONCERT VIBES & HIM

Ding! Ding! I had gotten a notification on my HBG app when I sat in the car. It was the same guy.

Hope I can see you sometime.

I closed out of the app and smiled at my cousin.

"Cousin, oh my God," I screeched with excitement, "today is finally concert day. Thanks for always being my concert buddy." I had hooked up my phone to her aux. I started playing my concert playlist.

"Mm-hmm. No problem," Dani stated, turning down the music, "Listen, Aiden Josiah. I am letting you know I am here. Jackson interrupted us earlier. I realized you didn't talk in front of Jackson and Terrence like that. There was something you want…"

"He raped me, Dani," I said with a cry out loud. As she talked, I understood she meant well. She only calls me Aiden Josiah when she is serious. I figured I had to tell her one part of what has been bothering me. I had to interrupt her. Luckily, when I had that outburst, we had come to a red light. She had hit the brakes so hard.

"Pull yourself together, because I am fine. I deal with it. Only Momo Jean and my mom knew. Now you are aware. It's just weird just being around Jim and seeing him be with Melissa."

She started trembling once I mentioned Jim and Melissa. "Ok, can we talk about this once we park?"

"Sure, Dani."

So she put the music back on. We stayed in traffic for an hour and fifteen minutes. We finally got to the fairgrounds so we could park and talk. There was police navigating traffic in parking. They directed us to our spot.

"Ok. Now that I'm settled," Danielle said. "What the fuck is going on?"

I huffed, "Ok, see, that is why I kept it to myself. The only people that knew were your Tee Joanne and Momo Jean. But Jim raped me, and I should have put him in jail when it happened, but I didn't. It's something I don't really like to discuss. Period."

"Ok, AJ. I am sorry if I made you feel you couldn't tell me about your pain," she said as her explanation, "But I'm here now. If it's painful to talk through, I understand. Though, I'm also trying to find out how Jim and Melissa get involved?"

"WELL, COUSIN," I said as a couple of tears rolled down my cheeks, "It happened. Jim was a member of Saint Mark Baptist Church in Marais Vert. I was 18. I was ashamed that I let this man violate me. He was someone who I trusted and looked up to as a father figure. I felt betrayed. He told me he would make sure alligators would eat up my body at Devil's Bayou if I told. I also figured that no one would believe me. Would believe me? Over a head deacon in the church? I told your Tee Joanne and Momo Jean. They believed me, and mom drove me to the ER. Unveiling the truth is what she wanted. But something inside me perceived protecting him would essentially protect me. So I lied to the doctor. I gave a false story about rough sex with a random hook-up. We never attended church again until after its tragedy. A shooting and a fire collectively destroyed the church in 2013. The community rebuilt it, installed a new pastor, and renamed it Agape Faith Baptist Church. That is the church my mom and I attend today."

DANIELLE REPLIED ANGRILY, "I wish I would have known. I really want to kill this piece of shit. But how in the hell did Melissa meet him?"

My breathing became heavy. I continued my interpretation. "After our incident, Jim apparently moved to New Orleans and started teaching at Weld NOLA Tech. Four years later, he saw our cousin riding the bull at The Swamp. He swept her off her feet with his financial status. So no one had knowledge of them eloping after three months, much less dating. So you remember when Momo and Mom acted out at Mel's Beauty Bar?"

"How can I forget Aiden," Dani said, following a snicker. "Momo tripped Jim with a cane. She played it off so well. Then her sweet voice saying, oh help me, Jesus. I'm sorry, sir."

"Well, that was because of me. Momo recognized him. So he smirked and told her we are family now with a smug smile. She was so enraged by his statement. She used her wit, knowing people would sympathize with her. That's when she tripped him. Mom was silent, but she had a knife in her purse. She wanted to stab him. However, she said to me that vengeance is mine, says the Lord. She hinted to Melissa everything glitters is not gold with that man. But of course, Melissa did not listen. All she saw was her cash cow and her dreams coming true."

"Well, now she is getting abused. You noticed she barely took her sunglasses off. She tried to cover that black eye with so much makeup. But if you were close to her, you could see it." She gave an explanation. "Well, shit! It's 12:30. I'm glad you opened up to me. I realize it took a lot of courage. We need to race to get into the VIP line."

"Yeah, cuz you right," I exhaled, "Before we go, can you pinky promise me you won't tell a soul? Jackson would want to kill, and Terrence would actually do it."

"I promise."

DANI GAVE A SMILE, and we locked pinkies. We hopped out of the car with our stuff and made a mad dash to the VIP line. We were optimistic about our luck. It seemed more people wanted to stay in their vehicles. They didn't want to wait in the scorching sun. They had barricades set up with three VIP lines and seven lines for general admission.

"We are not swiping in tickets to go inside until 2 PM," the female security guard said in a stern tone.

So we waited in the blistering sun. We did a little complaining. As more people started coming, we started getting bunched up. With 30 minutes left to go, Dani and I were facing forward. And then, BOOOM!

We turned around so quickly. Somebody behind us had passed out.

"Lord Jesus, it's already happening, and we ain't got inside yet," I said with a moan.

"I know, right? People usually start passing out two acts before Wayne," expressed Dani. She then said, "Somebody! Get a medic and some water, please!"

A male security guard came through our line with water. Another guard moved to the opposite side of the railings. They worked together to help the young lady over, and there was a 3rd security guard with a golf cart to take her to receive help.

"Cousin, please don't let me pass out. I don't wanna miss anything." I made a groan. "Keep me hydrated."

"Aw cousin, all these dudes out here. The boys should quench your thirst. Ya throat should not be dry," she said with a giggle.

I carried out a laugh. I thought to make a smart comment; the guard said in a loud voice, "It's 2:00. Listen up!"

He then instructed the other security guards out there; they spread out to all the lines. They let the VIP lines come in first after they checked us and gave us our bands. Soon, we ran through our section to our spots. We made it to the front like we always have. It's been our tradition for the past two years. An hour passed and the production crews were still setting up the stage. Then I felt it—the urge to tinkle.

"Dani, I gotta go."

"Boy, you better hurry back. People won't let you get your spot back. You know how these crowds work."

So I took off. I asked a short lady where the bathroom was. She pointed to them. They set them up like movie trailers and had wooden floors. They had a toilet, urinal, and a mirror with a chrome sink. It was so immaculate in there. I thought to myself; I was so glad we paid for VIP because the regular porter potties can be a disaster. Thoughts switched on how long and how warm it was after I used it and washed my hands.

Leaving out of the bathroom trailer, I entered this white tent. It was lit up with lights, like a circus tent. They had furniture set up where you could sit and a bar. I wasn't worried about drinks, though. I waited in the long line to get bottles of water. The workers yelled from the back as they ran out of ice. The only payments they were allowing were cash. Luckily, I had bills in my pocket. I ordered ten bottles of water. My thoughts raced faster than my feet were moving. I rushed to get my spot, and I dropped two bottles. He picked them up for me.

"Say, man, I got these, and give me three mo," he said with a thick island accent that made my heart flutter. "Oh, and I got you going through the crowd too."

"Thank you," I said in a murmur as I gave him the three.

So we both walked swiftly through the crowd. More people had come. But they didn't make it difficult for us to get back to our original spots. His girlfriend stood close enough to Dani. They were both facing us. She was a beautiful dark complexed girl standing at about 5 feet 4 inches.

"Dang, Jay. What took you so long?" She huffed as we were still squeezing through the crowd.

"I walked out of the bathroom. Little Homie, with all these water bottles, dropped some. I realized he was standing by us, so I helped him get back up here," he stated while he brushed his 5 feet 11 inches, 180-pound frame past my 5 feet 7 inches, 145-pound frame. I had a sensation of tingles in my spine, but I just stood there. Now we are standing side by side. The girls were in front of us. "Your name, bruh?"

"Oh, it's Aiden. Nice to meet you, Jay. And thanks for helping me," I said in a quiet tone. "This is my cousin, Danielle. Dani for short."

"It's nice to meet you, and this my girlfriend, Indigo. Indi for short," he replied, and winked at her.

"Well, give him his water because the show is starting," Indigo said in a commanding voice. She thought he had been too nice. He gave me the water bottles in which I told him to keep two for him and Indigo. He thanked me, then we paid attention to the platform. The host of the show had a towel, for he dripped in sweat. He created light jokes about how hot it was. It was scorching out there. With more people coming, pushing to see, I ended up between Indi and Dani. Jay was behind his girlfriend, holding her waist. I stared at him. He had brown dreads that were shoulder length. His eyes were a mesmerizing hazel on his smooth bronze complexion. I hadn't noticed I was gazing until…

Indigo makes a sarcastic cough. "You ok? Something in your eye?" she asked.

I just ignored her and whispered to Dani to switch places. She obliged. That's when the show started.

THE FIRST ACT was Akbar V from Atlanta. I had never heard of her before, but I loved her energy. She was getting power from the crowd, mostly on our side of the stage. She moved back and forth in an Atlanta Braves jersey and blue jean shorts. The lyrics she rapped were what I call fire bars. She even did her dancing in some fresh white kicks. She performed the last song, which delighted the crowd. It made the crowd hyper and dance. She shook all that rump to the beat. I had to join in and shake my little buns; still, I sensed eyes watching me.

The next act was Leven Kali from Los Angeles. He had on this open sheer pink shirt and a white tee with his maroon sweatpants. The vocals and vibes he gave were calming. Dani poked me when he came to our side. "What about his hair?"

"Girl, I love that color."

She scrunched up her face. I recognized her liking his vibes, but not that hair color. I could only laugh at her while she shrugged.

Then after him, Vice Versa, a rap duo, performed. Lil Twist followed them. I bobbed my head so hard. I noticed Jay's reaction to the stage out of the corner of my eye. By this time, I was positioned behind Dani next to him.

"You know nothing about this music. Little Homie tryna be down." Jay had produced a small laugh.

All I could do was poke my lips because he was right.

THE NEXT ARTIST TO come to the platform whose music I appreciated was Kash Doll. It was like I came alive. When her DJ came speaking on the mic, I got hype. I was moving so fast, putting my charger on my phone to record her doing my favorite songs by her. Kash had a fuchsia-colored bodysuit that hugged her body and matching heels. Dani and I screamed so loud when she performed her songs "Check" and "Run Me My Money". She whipped her blonde bob, dancing and rapping with us. The highlight for us was Lil Wayne's daughter, Reginae, coming out and performing "For Everybody" with Kash Doll. She did it so well in her black outfit, flipping her blue hair.

Dani nudged me when they finished and told me to look over. I did, and Jay and Indi didn't look like they were having fun. I felt terrible for him.

Then Dani said with a yell, "YASSSS SAWEETIE!!!!"

Saweetie came performing her song "High Maintenance". Dani just took her excitement to the next level, hollering. She rhymed every single word. I rocked to and loved the choreography from her dancers, who were wearing red 05 mid-drift tanks and mesh shorts with red drawers. Saweetie rocked a white bandana on her head and her icy chain. The crowd enjoyed her as she strutted back and forth, donning a black and white FUBU midriff shirt and shorts set. Now, while she performed "Icy Grl" and "My Type", I looked over. Indi danced with Jay. I guess she is picky with who she likes musically. His reaction was non-existent.

THE NEXT ARTIST got everyone smiling. Megan Thee Stallion. One of the newest raptress in the rap game, she made her way to the stage performing "Realer". You could hear everyone outside. I looked back at the crowd packed to capacity. The braids to ponytail hairstyle were intricate in her hair. She stunned us in that purple outfit with a black bra and fishnet stockings. She interacted with the crowd and entertained us with "Cocky AF", "Neva", and "Sex Talk". All four of us had a moment where we were having fun. I mean, the energy was insane. Then, her dancers came wearing black bras with a sheer gray top. But I loved their fishnets with the chrome bottoms. She and they then performed "Freak Nasty", "Hot Girl Summer", and "Cash Shit". I was so pleased with her performance. The next part of her show was the crowd participation segment. She picked people from the crowd, including Dani, to get on stage and dance. I was too excited. Reginae even joined on stage and danced. I had to record. My cousin even got to dance to "Big Ole Freak". That was the highlight of the night.

"Aiden, Puh-lease tell me you got me dancing," Dani said with a plea.

"Yes, Cousin. I can't wait to show our people when you get home," I said with a chuckle.

"Say, Dani, you did good," Jay said.

"And why are you doing the most?" asked Indigo.

"Man, look. Wah mek a yuh acting lakka that?" Jay asked her, "Mi cyaan compliment nobody?"

She didn't have a response. I didn't have one either. But Jay sounded sexy when he was mad. I was daydreaming about his accent. Suddenly, the next act came to the stage.

Enter Trey Songz, who came out to the platform performing "Invented Sex". The 90-degree weather was not the only thing causing the girls to sweat. Jay rolled his eyes. Trey looked excellent in his blue and red collared shirt. He wore a white tee with a picture of young Wayne on it, matched with light denim jeans. He mesmerized the girls and sang "Neighbors Know My Name".

"Indi girl, that Trey is some fine," Dani expressed.

"Guh, he is. And it is Indigo," Indigo replied quickly.

"Man. When is he getting off the stage?" Jay butted in.

"Sounds like you hatin', sir," I responded.

"Man, I ain't got to trip," Jay spoke.

I shushed him, "He singing 'Dive In'."

He was holding Indigo by her waist. "Man, I wanna dive into something tonight." Then he looks at me and licks his lips.

He needs to stop playing with me. Those were my exact thoughts. Suddenly, Trey had just taken his shirt off. The girls started screaming in octaves that could have busted my eardrums. Trey journeyed through songs like "Heart Attack" and transitioned from that to "Say Aah". Then I got loud when the band started "Bottoms Up". I scared everybody when I started jumping. It felt like everyone who bought a ticket was here. We packed the space like sardines in a tiny can. I sang the whole song, especially Nicki Minaj's verse.

MEEK MILL WAS UP NEXT. Now, Jay didn't fangirl, but he played it cool, his excitement at seeing Meek. Personally, I was just waiting for him to perform my favorite songs that I liked. The crowd's energy did kick up a notch as he entertained in a green tee and denim jeans. He iced his neck with his Dreamchasers' chains. I turned to look at Jay.

That man recited every word. Indigo was popping it on him. She turned her head, looking to see if Dani was paying attention. I thought she was a beautiful girl, but to be so insecure is crazy. We all became crazy when Meek introduced "House Party". Then he announced "24/7". Dani and I did our little rocking-away shoulders dance. Jay heard "Going Bad" and rhymed to it. Meek performed some more hits: "I'm a Boss", "All Eyes on You", and "Dreams & Nightmares". The latter two being my favorite Meek songs.

So they had a small intermission. Travis Scott was the last artist to perform before Wayne. We had been there the entire day. The time read 9 o'clock on my cellular. People were getting restless. We bunched together like the rest of the spectators along with us. People were steadily pushing, trying to get to the front. While Travis was performing, he stopped because someone fainted from heat exhaustion. He was great about making sure fans were straight before he continued his part of the show. Those ten bottles I had bought for the entire day had dwindled to four. His special effects on the screens and his pyrotechnics were significant. Donning a black tee and pants with stars on them, he performed the three songs I recognized the most: "Antidote", "Butterfly Effect", and "Goosebumps".

As soon as Travis walked off the stage, I gave two of the four bottles to Jay. "Here, I don't want y'all passing out around me."

"Thanks, Man. You real cool."

MY FACE WAS BLUSHING. Indigo wasn't paying any concern; she was just watching for Wayne. Then a DJ started playing "6 foot 7 foot".

Wayne appeared in a white tee and a backward cap. His jeans were so unique with animals, letters, and numbers stitched to them. Jay was bobbing his head hard to "No Worries". The entire crowd was enjoying the show. People continued passing out like flies around us because of dehydration. Security helped plenty of people over the barricades. Wayne highlighted a few hits like "Lollipop", "Miss Officer", and "Bitches Love Me". He even brought out Gudda Gudda to perform "Bedrock". Wayne brought out many special guests during his set for them to play their music. Cheeky Black, Wacko and Skip, Choppa, Future, and DJ Khaled all hit the stage. Man, the intensity at the concert elevated. When Wayne would perform, I realized how long I was listening to him. His discography is lengthy but notable. He ended the show at around 30 minutes to midnight.

All four of us were sweaty and exhausted. We were pushing through the lines very slow. We heard a commotion. The next thing I noticed, it was just Dani and me together. We were holding hands, making sure we kept track of each other. It disheartened me. I didn't at least try to get Jay's number because he was a neat guy.

We finally arrived at the car. Dani could sense something that disappointed me.

"AJ, I'm glad we went. Memories we made will last a lifetime. You ok?" she asked.

"Yeah, cousin. I'm just sad I didn't have time to say goodbye to Jay. He was a real cool dude. I wonder if we will ever meet again," I pondered.

"Nigga. He had a girlfriend. Capital on the G I R L, and that girl is something. Cousin, you will be fine," she replied. My notification to HBG sounded. "See what I mean. Answer your app."

"Guh, you are so nosy and messy for that," I whined as a snicker shrieked out of my mouth. As Dani drove us to Jack in the Box and home, I checked my new message. It was from that mysterious guy.

So, I know the concert let out. You gave me "Fever" in your shirt. Hope we can link up.

Wait. What? You mean to tell me that mysterious guy was at the concert. My thoughts were racing. That is when I wondered if he was Jay.

4

SUNDAY & THE LAKEFRONT

"Aye, wake your ass up," Jackson says, "Oops. I am sorry, Lord. Kind sir, can you get up, please?"

I opened my eyes. My cousin was standing over me with black slacks and dress socks on. That could mean one thing. It's time to get ready for church. The thoughts of going to church flooded my brain with different emotions. One thing I sensed was tiredness from the concert last night. The other matter was enjoying service but without Momo Jean.

"Jack, I love you. However, I am not going," I said.

Jackson clears his throat. "Ok," he replied. He snuck off into the restroom. Not a minute after, my phone rings on the charger.

"Hello?"

"Aiden Josiah Phillips. I understand how you feel. But, you need to embrace your new normal. Momo Jean will always be with you. So get your behind up for church. Don't make me drive down there and drag you to the church house. I will be in New Orleans before you blink. Don't play with me. Did I make myself clear?" My mom said in an authoritative tone.

Ugh! Why did he rat? I was sure I didn't wish to go to church now. I realized I better get dressed. Joanne would be down here and pull me by ears to praise God.

I got up, passing the bathroom door. "Snitch!"

I could pick up Jackson's laugh behind the door. I returned to the living room. My mind was playing tricks on me. I couldn't remember where I put my dressy attire. I searched through my luggage and got my dress clothes. Jack was coming out of the restroom. He called out, "Cuz. You got time. It's only 9:30. We gonna make it for the 11 o'clock service."

"Alright," I said back in a yell so he could hear me. I took a shower and got dressed. I felt light and ready, with gray slacks and a cerulean blue shirt. When I got out of the bathroom, Dani was standing there waiting for me.

"Boy, you take as much time in the shower as I do," she cooed.

"Well, I had to clean my wee-wee," I said with a chuckle.

She screamed with a loud cackle, "You make me sick! You are some childish. Not on this good Sunday. I'm glad I ain't put my makeup on. I would smear my mascara, dying laughing at you. Let me in this bathroom crazy."

I got my stuff and moved back into the living room. Jack came out of his room. "Even though I had to call Tee Joanne on you, I am truly glad you're coming to church," he said with a soft smile.

"Me too," I smirked. "I noticed I was dressed. You have your clothes, and Dani is showering. So, where is Terrence? Why is he not coming?"

"Terrence is going to watch TBN like he always does. He did that when Momo was alive. What would Momo say? He is getting the word. That matters. I see what point you are trying to make. Look at this picture of our grandmother. She would want you to face your fear and trust God. She is in your head and heart. That's why Y-O-U are stepping foot in that church house," he said, giving his justification.

I cried because I understood what he said and meant was true. I had so many memories of Momo Jean in her all-white suit. Her love for God was the reason she was a doorkeeper of his house. Looking up at her photo, I nodded. I realized it meant I was going. Twenty minutes later, Dani was wearing her powdered blue dress, Jackson had made his teal shirt perfect, and I was emotionally ready to go.

WE GOT into Jack's 2017 all-black Chevrolet Camaro and were at Agape Faith 10 minutes to the 11 o'clock hour. As we walked in, it felt safe and euphoric, like home. We sat on the 5th pew in the back; it was on the left side. By the 3rd hymnal, I identified relaxation and being uplifted. Then I made a huge mistake. The door was opening; I turned to view who was coming into the sanctuary. It was them.

Jim and Melissa Daniels. First, I felt tricked by God and Momo Jean. They barely go to church. Their first stepping into a church house since they had got married was when Momo died. I was over it. Jim had on a tan suit with matching loafers. Melissa matched him with a dress with heels. I locked eyes with her for a quick second and turned around, facing forward. So they sat in the pew behind us.

"Hello, family," Melissa tried to speak in such an innocent manner. I had too many bottled-up emotions inside to talk. I knew I was in the house of the Lord, but I also knew my mouth. So I kept quiet.

"Uh, Melissa. It's good to see you in church," Jack replied.

"Yeah, she brought the devil in here," Dani said, with a mumble under her breath. I elbowed her arm. "Ouch."

"What you said, Dani?" Melissa asked. Jim gave her a stern expression for her to drop her questioning.

"I said, oh, it's good that you came," Dani spat back.

"I thought so," Melissa said with her smug remark. Jim pinched her, and she stopped speaking before trying to make me talk.

The choir started singing, and the ushers got into their formation. I sighed because it was offering time. My favorite thing was seeing Momo Jean strut down the aisle. The congregation walked around; I walked to the bathroom afterward. So I wash my hands after going and in walks Mr. Jim Daniels. So I turned around. I could barely stand the sight of this man. Standing 6 feet 4 inches, 250 pounds, he had a devious look on his face as he entered the bathroom. I gagged as I smelled the woodsy cologne that reminded me of what he did to me.

"You look really well."

"Please stay away from me," I said in an unforgiving voice. "You shouldn't stare at me or try to touch me. I'm not that scared young man anymore. I will scream."

"That would be a sweet sound to my ears."

"You are sick," I said. I was so disgusted. Before he could come anymore close to me, the lights flickered in the bathroom. He looked at me as if he was looking past me. He detected something in the mirror that made his jaw drop. It made him hurry out of the bathroom. I turned to see what he saw. However, all I caught sight of was me. I shrugged my shoulders. I exited back into the sanctuary; Jim and Melissa had already left, though. It puzzled me.

"Dani, what happened to your cousin and her husband?" I asked.

"I'll tell you after church," Dani said in a whisper. Jackson snickered not only at that situation. The old soloist had tried to hit a high note, but it fell flat.

After that, Pastor Fredrick McKee was standing at the podium. He titled the message: "God helps us face our fears". I rolled my eyes and looked up at the heavens. My thoughts were I had been set up. Pastor Fredrick had a way with words. He preached his points on how God will help us in our time of being fearful. He related the stories of David & Goliath and Moses & the Red Sea to make his point. I was sobbing. His message was what I needed to hear.

GOSPEL MUSIC PLAYED on the way home. We stopped at Wendy's, grabbing us all something to eat. When we got home & up the stairs, I hadn't forgotten that my question didn't receive an answer.

"So who is telling what happened to Jim and Melissa at church?" I asked.

"Shush! Peace be still, you discipline," Jack said as a joke.

"Now you know it's disciple you meant to say." I made a chuckle.

"Cuz, we will tell you as soon as we get out these clothes. Plus, we gotta give Big T the scoop too."

"Ok." So I go through my luggage, and I take my Aeropostale blue tee shirt and jeans to the bathroom. As I'm getting dressed, I hear that specific notification noise that I recognize all too well. I run back to get my phone. The message was from the mysterious guy.

Meet me at the lakefront at 10:30 tonight.

I messaged back. *Ok.*

I heard footsteps coming from the back. "Man, what up, Cousin?"

It was Terrence. He came and sat by me on the couch.

"Man, Cuz. Nothing much, man. I am waiting for your brother and Dani to finish getting comfortable. We saw your favorite cousin today."

"Man, that's YOUR cousin," he emphasized. "I don't fuck with that jealous bitch, brah. Real talk. Everybody in this family knows that. She was always jealous of us 4. And especially you. Wait, sorry, Lord. You saw her? Not at the church, huh?"

"Yep, I know, cuz. It surprised me too, and she had her husband with her. I was like, Lord, do devils want to repent? But she is our cousin. At the day's end, she has our blood."

"Well, shit. Sorry, Lord. I can't wait to hear DJ play this gospel record."

"I caught that one, Big T. Cute. And push over," Dani sweetly gave Terrence a command, with Jackson following behind her. "So Aiden Josiah, why did you scare that man? Be honest."

I started rubbing my hands together. "I did nothing to him. Frankly, I told him he shouldn't stare at me. I told him he should stay away from me. So what happened?"

Jackson cackled, "Man, he came back scared. His eyes were like bucked open. Then he looked pale. Like somebody sucked the life out of him pale. I couldn't laugh because I was in church. Now..."

He started laughing louder. Dani turned and gave him a severe gaze. That made him quiet down.

"AJ, Jim basically looked like he saw a ghost when he came back. Jackson said that he was looking pale and scared," she furthered her explanation. "He nervously was tapping Melissa on the shoulder to get up. Of course, she wanted to stay. He started pulling her arm lightly as if to say, I will leave you here. So she got up, and they left."

The possibilities rolled through my head, but I said nothing. I wondered what he got a glimpse of in that mirror behind me. I said nothing to my family because maybe it wasn't worth mentioning.

"Hello, Earth," Dani said. She snapped her fingers at me to get my attention. I had been daydreaming. "Seems like you were in a daze. What are you thinking about?"

"Well, y'all. I don't know. I mean, I was just satisfied he was out of my face."

"Mm-hmm. I am aware." She had a grin on her face. "But that happened. I still wonder what spooked him."

Terrence said in a bellow, "Let's change the subject. So y'all know I'm a big playa, ya know."

We started laughing as he talked.

He said, "But y'all, I think I am ready to settle down. While you guys were at church, I invited a young lady over to praise and chill."

"Praise and chill?" I screamed. "What the? Please explain this one to me."

Dani and Jack made it no better. They were over there cackling like hens, waiting for this explanation.

"Well, Cuz. It's when you invite a date over to watch the church service with you," he gave his description, "You talk about life and the Lord. So I invited this young lady over. We watched the service together, reflect on today's message, and talk about life. Her name is Evette. I want you guys to meet her."

Jack goes to touch his brother on the forehead like he is feeling for a temperature. "Well, he is doing fine. I mean, maybe he smoked too much weed. It has clouded his judgment. Normally, I can't meet his girls."

Even Terrence had to laugh. "Mane, look, I'm serious, ya know. I really like her."

"Well, one thing about my cousin, he likes her. He was that way, growing up always. When he likes a girl, he says, ya know, over and over," Dani says, stating the obvious.

"Man, y'all teasing me, and I'm serious, ya know," Terrence expressed.

"Y'all leave my cousin alone," I said. "I am excited about meeting this chick. Whatever makes you content, Cuz. So when we meet her?"

"For Regina's birthday party. October 19. Side note, though…"

I perceived there was a catch. My ears got ready to listen to this explanation.

"I was rocking with her three years. Momo told me something before she died. I would get into a relationship with that young lady. I called all my female friends, and she was the only one who briefly came to Momo's funeral. Tired of playing with other women. I want to be great for her," he disclosed.

"Well, I believe my cousin—many blessings. I can't wait to meet Evette," I expressed.

We all smiled at him and started family time. We started playing pitty-pat, Uno, and spades for bragging rights. I lost all the pitty-pat games, of course. Then I got my respect back, playing everyone with Uno. While we were on our fifth game of 5 card draw, Dani's text notification sounded.

"Uh, Aiden, you gotta be spending the night again. It's 11:00. Tee Joanne just texted me."

Shit! Up, I hopped. Thank God, in between games, I had been packing my clothes. I went to check my phone. It was still silent from when we attended church. I texted my mom right away after seeing all the voicemails and text messages. Then I read a couple of messages from the mysterious guy still wanting to see him. I grabbed all my stuff.

"Alright, y'all. Love y'all." I gave dap to Terrence and Jackson. Dani followed me out.

"You not going straight home, are you?" Dani asked.

"No, I am not. I'm going to go meet up with somebody first," I said.

"You better be careful, and of course, I will not rat you out."

"Thank you," I said with a laugh. We pinky swore, as we always did.

~

So I HOPPED in the car and plugged my phone up. I messaged the mysterious guy.

Hey. I am tired, but I can meet you wherever you want in 20 minutes.

He responded: *Meet me at the lakefront.*

I put my GPS and my Weezyana playlist on. My head was bopping and concentrating. I thought I had learned about the city's streets by now, but nope. That GPS was guiding me straight to my destination. So I parked and let him know what model car I drive.

I'm just jamming to the music, waiting for him to drive up.

Tap. Tap. Tap.

I whipped my head from dancing, and I rolled my window down. He bent down, and that's when I saw him.

"My name is Shamar," he said with a thick island accent, "you mind if I sit and chat with you?"

"I'm Aiden, and sure, no problem," I stated. I was eager, but I didn't want to seem too keen. So I unlocked the door. He walked smoothly around to the passenger side. As he opened the door, I adjusted my seat to make sure he was at ease.

He was the definition of tall, dark, and handsome. He was wearing an all-black Adidas suit as I looked into his honey brown eyes. My admiration made him uneasy.

"So, you mesmerized by looks? I mean, I see you staring," he said, "Huh?"

I was too busy staring at his lips that looked soft. Finally, I looked up from his lips to his eyes.

"Hey, I'm sorry. When I'm attracted to someone's face and voice, I stare unintentionally," I admittedly said.

"Well, I'm half Jamaican and half African-American. Yuh cool. And cute too." He had the prettiest grin I saw.

I blushed. I definitely felt my cheeks getting rosy.

"Do you think we can drive to my favorite spot?" He asked. I nodded my head. He directed me to drive around to a particular spot. We were still on the lakefront, but a unique part. We parked.

"Cum pan."

"What?" I asked.

"Come on."

So we got out of the car; he took me by the hand softly. It scared me at first because holding hands with a guy in public like this still gets its stares today. But as we walked hand in hand, I relaxed. We sat on this bench in front of a water fountain. It was so peaceful watching it.

For 2 hours, we talked, and I learned we shared quite a few common interests. We both enjoyed watching Card Sharks, NCIS, and any show on the ID channel. Our favorite sports to watch are football and tennis. He enjoys reading books and listening to music as much as I do. Fried chicken, specifically from Popeye's, is our favorite food.

But when talks turned personal, he wanted to learn about me and my life. I shared with him how I was a customer rep at an AT&T store and how I loved my job. I also told him how I wanted to open an online jewelry store. It intrigued him how goal-oriented I was.

When it was time for him to share, he gave me limited information about himself. It was like his life was a touchy subject. Family and friends were topics not discussed with me. With education, he kind of opened up. He told me he went to Tulane for psychology, but he switched programs and schools and dropped out the mid-semester in October last year. He steered clear of divulging deeper into that.

It was around 1:30 AM; I had yawned because of tiredness.

"I see you tired. You should go home," Shamar said.

"I am tired, but you think I could sleep at your place?" I asked.

"Hell nuh," he said with a quickness. "I mean no man. I stay with my mom and brother."

"It's cool," I replied. I was so sleepy, so I knew I had to get home.

"We will link up again. And don't even ask about dropping me off. I'm getting an Uber. So go," he stated.

"You promise?" I wondered.

He gave me a warm kiss with stiff lips on my forehead.

"I promise," he assured me. We got up, and he walked me to the car. He gave me dap. "Come on, man. Message me when you get home."

"Ok," I said.

So I pulled off, put my music on, and headed home. While I was driving, I would blink fast. It seemed like something, or someone, was making sure I stayed up and alert. Soon as I pulled into the yard, he messaged me if I made it. I answered him yep and got my stuff. I got up to the door. My hands fumbled with my key in the lock. I got it open and crept into the house. My mother was on the couch sleep with her mouth wide open. If I had time, I would have taken a picture; that is how we prank each other. So I just tip-toed and got into my room, making minimal noise without waking her.

"Ahh," I exhaled as I spread across my bed. I fell fast asleep, dreaming about the next time I would see Shamar.

5

WORK AND PINING FOR SOME ATTENTION

"Wake your ass up," my mother said to me. She made sure it was a yell. My eardrums hurt from her fussing. I never checked the time before turning my back. "Your ass shouldn't come to my house so late. You know damn well you gotta be up for work."

I appreciated my mom. I really did. However, I was so groggy; all I wanted to do was sleep. It was 7:30 in the morning.

WAP!!!

"Oh My God, Joanne!" I said as she slapped one of my legs. I made a yelp because that slap hurt. She had the determination for me to get out of bed by any means necessary.

"Get your ass up! I ain't gonna tell you again."

"Fine," I said in an indistinct murmur. "I am going to call them, alright. I'm going to tell them I'm not coming."

"The hell you are. You are going to that job. You should have come back home earlier instead of lollygagging with the family."

In my head, I chuckled as loud as I could. Dani and I only had information on my whereabouts. So I did everything necessary to get myself fixed for work. Luckily, I had an outfit hung up in the closet ready. I dressed and braced to run out the door. My mother was right. She understood I hated to be tardy.

"Here," she said, handing me my keys as I rushed out the door. "And whenever you get home, I wanna learn about this young man. He kept you out all night."

"Mama, how yo-?" I said, letting out a small gasp.

"Boy, bye. I know my child. Plus, I have a mother's intuition. Now beat it."

I CLOSED the door behind me, and I got in my car. My music got boosted up to keep me awake while I was driving. I arrived in the parking lot of the AT&T call center with 10 minutes to spare. So I hurried to the bathroom; then I unlocked my locker to put up and lock away my valuables. Once I made it to the floor, I clocked in on time. I passed the check-in desk.

"Whoa! Come back, Mr. Phillips," a familiar husky voice said.

It was Mrs. Aurora Bush. She was my 57-year-old Caucasian supervisor. She had her hands on hefty hips as she was about 210 pounds, but stood at my height.

"So tell me how your weekend was real quick?"

"Well, Mrs. Bush, I had fun with my family. The concert was great. It was fun. I especially loved when Megan and Trey Songz performed. Those were my highlights," I stated.

"Oh, ok, that is so wonderful." She wanted to carry on the conversation. But she knew I had to log in and start taking calls. "Well, my grandson attended the show, and he had fun, too. His favorite part was Meeky Mills."

"Meek Mill."

"Yeah, that is him. Anyway, I will tell you later how he felt about the concert. You can go ahead to your station now."

I didn't even say thank you. I sprinted to my computer. My fingers typed my login so quickly; I made it in time.

Now I loved my job, but sometimes I hated it. It was a hassle getting cursed out by customers of all races and languages. It is not my fault some of humanity can be irresponsible in paying their bill. But I always showed sympathy; you never realize what people go through. My favorite type of call was new service orders. They were the easiest for me to process. Also, I honestly believed in the products I was selling. I was on a call when somebody tapped my chair.

It was Eliza. Soon there was a message telling me to take my break. So as I walked like I always do, everybody giggled on their calls.

"I wonder why everybody laughed when I passed?" I asked once I made it to the break room and sat with her.

"That's because Speedy Gonzales, you walk so fast all we see is your blue shirt in a blur. Not only that, we hear the swish in your pants," Eliza had a nice joke, "so real quick, tell me about the concert. Like I saw, you were really close. I didn't have time to text you. You were on Tidal in the crowd."

"Wait, girl, are you serious?"

"Yes, I will show you the pics on lunch break. Ugh, it's time to go back."

"These breaks be going by too fast."

"Yep." She nodded and fled back to the work floor. I had a few seconds to think. So I texted Shamar on the app. I proceeded to my locker, got my phone, and sent him a text just saying hi. When I entered the restroom, I felt rushed. I put away my phone after exiting it. My mind focused on work, walking to the floor. It made me better at times, more fun processing my client's calls.

I was ready to clock out for lunch. It was 1 PM, and I was fit to eat. I made my way to my locker to get my cell. I checked the HBG app. Shamar still did not message me. I got annoyed, but I calmed my temper. I got a call from my Waitr guy he was here. We met at the front door.

"Thank you," I stated, handing him an extra $5 tip.

"Your welcome," he replied as he handed me my food. It was a chicken shawarma salad and a Lebanese tea from Albasha, a Greek and Lebanese restaurant in Baton Rouge. So I sat down to eat. Eliza, Bonita, and Glenn entered from the work floor into the break room.

Eliza said as a suggestion, "Aiden, we are always eating well." Earlier, she had ordered a steak medium-rare, a baked potato, and a blooming onion from Outback Steakhouse.

"That is true," I said with enthusiasm. "Bonita, what you have?"

"Oh, nothing too fancy, just a Popeyes chicken sandwich," she said in a murmur, lowering her eyes. Bonita was my shy work friend. She is what you will call a quiet worker bee.

"Girl, lift them brown eyes. I eat Popeyes too. Hell, when it's the day before payday, I scrape up my pennies just to buy myself a cheeseburger at McDonald's. But one day, I'll buy your lunch too."

She looked up and smiled. She had a beautiful set of brown eyes that matched her cocoa brown skin.

"I could never get so hungry to eat McDonald's. I would call my parents and have them order me something like Olive Garden or Ruth Chris. McDonald's, Taco Bell, and Burger King. Yuck! My palate is too rich for that," Eliza said with a snicker, seriously flipping her raven-colored hair.

Bonita and I had to laugh at her. Eliza could be pretty comical.

So we ate. It dawned on Eliza that she had not shown me the screenshot pictures from Tidal. So they got me talking about the concert, and I started laughing, telling the story of my cousin's reaction to Saweetie.

"Humph. What's so funny?" A shady voice began.

"Glenn, why on earth are you mad at every reaction I make?"

He got up from where he sat, coming towards our table. "That is because you are so fake. Didn't your grandma die not too long ago? And you are here laughing and talking? Chile, spare me."

"You are so miserable. You're pushing my buttons, and I have done nothing too. Don't you ever speak on Momo, and please leave me alone," I stated.

Eliza and Bonita both gasped. He walked away like he completed a mission to get under my skin.

I felt like he was baiting me. I had no idea. Why for what? I wasn't mean when I said it. I hated being picked on and needed to defend myself. That is the one thing I remembered Momo Jean telling me in her last conversations with her.

SHE HAD BEEN to my house in her room. We had just finished watching the Y&R as we always did. She turned to me and said, "Listen. Aiden. I want to tell you I love you."

"Aww, I love you too, Momo Jean."

"Now, I wasn't there." Momo Jean said to express regret. "I recognize I was not there to protect you from that heathen. In my own ways afterward, I was there. I always will be when I pass. Two things you need to do for yourself though. With the Lord's help, of course."

"I know, Momo. Don't cry. But what you need me to do?"

"I need you to forgive, and I also need you to stand up for yourself."

"Momo!"

"Listen, Josiah. Like I said, your mother and I will not be on this earth forever. You are so good at trying to make everyone happy. Put yourself first sometimes. It is ok to be assertive. Sometimes folk will seek to use you just because you are a nice and loving person. People decide to take advantage of you. They do that now. Well, at least I hope not. You must watch the company you are around. Others might not fancy you are full of joy all the time. You have a light. Let nobody dim it. But also forgive them who hurt you; that is what the 'Good Book' says."

"Momo, for you, I will work on it."

"That's my AJ."

WHEN I LOOKED UP, I recognized I was about to be late heading back. Some 1:30 lunch crew members had received their lunch message early. I threw my trash away, put my phone in my locker, took care of my bathroom needs, and dashed down the hall. I clocked back in on time.

While walking to my seat, I realized I still didn't get a response from Shamar. I tried to play it cool. However, that kind of thing bothers me, and I think the worst. To distract me from my thoughts, I dove into work. The phones rang so much. I ended up working over my break time. I sped off to the restroom once they sent the break message to me. Rushing to my locker, I couldn't open it. I wanted to go back to work. After three tries, I popped it open, got my phone, and still no message from Shamar.

I slammed my locker door and locked it. Everybody could tell something was wrong; they had never seen me like this. I thought that he could have at least texted me a damn hello. Steam felt like it was coming out of my ears. I walked back early and logged into my station. My last two hours of work progressed well for the rest of my shift.

Before I could get up, I heard a familiar unpleasant laugh.

"See you tomorrow, Aiden," Glenn said with a sinister grin.

"Hmm. It's going to be one hell of a week." I said to myself in a mumble.

I almost commented on his appearance. He was 5 feet 4 inches, the color of a steak burned past well done and shaped like Humpty Dumpty. However, if I would try to down him, then I would have stooped to his level. I was not for that.

I finally got up and walked casually to my locker. My locker opened. I counted to ten, picked up my phone. Yet, there was still no notification.

"Hey, I'm not aware of Glenn getting to you. It's going to be ok. Plus, it's a new day tomorrow," Eliza said, trying to cheer me up.

"Thanks. See you tomorrow," I nodded.

"See you tomorrow."

So I GRABBED my phone and headed out the door. I thought that today wasn't so bad. When I got in the car, I put on my R&B playlist. It has the music of the likes of Joe,

Fantasia, Jazmine Sullivan, and more. My headspace was in that vibe. I started questioning myself in my head about how I would handle being ignored. It hurts my feelings deeply when I feel that way.

The commute wasn't horrible, but midway through the drive, thunderstorms came. I hate driving in the rain. When I pulled up, I thanked God for living in a house with a carport. As soon as I walked into the house, I could smell the food. I didn't realize I was hungry until now. Joanne fixed me a nice plate, and we sat at our little table. I looked over at that empty chair where Momo Jean used to sit. As I was about to cry, my mother grabbed my hands.

"Let me say grace."

"Sure, mom."

"Lord, thank you for the food. Let it be nourishing to our bodies. Thank you for the preparer and for those eating. P.S. Father, we miss your servant, my mother. Help her watch over us in Jesus's name. Amen."

"Amen."

So we sat there and ate. Man, that food was nutritious. She cooked the corn, peas, and baked chicken, just as Momo Jean cooked it.

"So, Aiden, how was work? Better yet! Tell the truth. What young man kept you out? You know the other night?" Joanne stated. I knew she was buttering me up with food, only to be nosy.

I laughed.

"And what's so funny?" she mocked.

"Ok, mom. Work was fine. A coworker made a remark, but I told him to leave me alone." I loved how nosy my mother was being. My laughing escaped my head and came out. "As far as the young man, he was ok, but he is a flake."

"I told you about the boys who like to fuck and duck."

"MAMA!" I screamed and cackled so loud that I scared her.

"What?" she said. She shrugged and smiled. "I'm just saying."

I got our plates and washed the dishes. Laughter escaped my lips. I mean, it was the least that I could do. After I washed up, I got ready for bed early. Today had been a day. I now knew what to expect.

My phone rang.

"Guh, what you want?" I asked cheerfully.

"Well, I wanted to know if my favorite cousin was coming down this weekend? After work, of course," she replied.

Ugh, Danielle could convince me to come down to the city anytime. I loved spending time with her. It is always a pick me up being around her.

"Ok," I made a groan, "I guess I will come down. So what will we be doing?"

"That part I am keeping a surprise," she said with a giggle. "Trust me. See you after work Saturday."

Then she hung up in my face.

Danielle knows me so well. She knew I was going to ask 20 million questions or pester her. All I could do was laugh.

Ding! Ding!

I got a notification. To my surprise, it was from Shamar.

Hey, I'm sorry I am just getting to you. I really apologize. I hope I see you sometime Saturday.

I messaged him. *Ok. I'll text you when I'm down.*

He sent a smiley face back. Did he know I was traveling down to the city? I pondered and scratched my head and questioned myself. Maybe he has ESP or something. I laughed it off as a coincidence. My thought was this upcoming weekend sounded interesting. I turned over and went to sleep.

6

A BOURBON STREET GETAWAY & A READING

The rest of my work week happened with no significant blowups. Of course, Glenn got on my nerves occasionally. But I never acted out of character. I was not allowing him to bring me to that place again.

Earlier this week, I made a request to Mrs. Aurora. I desired to work from 7 AM to 3:30 PM and take off Sunday. Usually, they would have denied it, but I would be fine as long as I worked the following Saturday.

So it was 11 o'clock, and I was taking my lunch break. I led myself to the vending machine, got myself a sandwich, and sat down. It just so happened that Bonita, Eliza, and Glenn received their first break. What struck my eyes when they strolled up was Eliza. She wore this gorgeous knee-length dress that was sea green. It matched her apricot skin as she strutted my way.

"Someone got here early to leave earlier," Eliza remarked.

"I had to because of plans with my cousin. It was luck," I replied.

"Special treatment," Glenn coughed in a mumble.

Before I could even utter a word, Eliza looked him dead in his eyes. Her hazel green met his dark brown. "Can you please?"

"Humph," he shrugged and wandered off.

"What is with him?"

"I don't know. I don't have a clue."

Coming out of her shell, Bonita asked curiously, "So, what do you and cousin have planned, Aiden?"

"Girl, she did not tell me, so I am excited."

Eliza elbowed her slightly. "Mm-hmm, come on, Bonita, before we are late getting back. Aiden, you better inform us all about the trip."

"Gotcha. I will."

And they headed back in. I completed eating my sandwich but realized I had not checked my cell. I opened my locker and reviewed my message after throwing my trash away.

Hey, cousin. My first surprise is that I bought ourselves a room. It is at the hotel of your dreams. Meet me there when you get off. Love U, Dani.

OH SHIT! I was getting excited. A slight smile was occurring across my face. I put my phone up and took care of my needs. I left back to the call floor.

Mrs. Bush stopped me in my tracks.

"I observed your smile. I am glad I could get you off. Now, don't make this a habit."

She spoke it so firmly to where I recognized she hinted she did me a favor. All I could do was nod my head and go sit at my station.

For the rest of the day, the clients gave me the blues. They were cussing me out, complaining about the bills and their lines, and, not to mention, my favorite, asking for discounts. I realized I had to keep my composure. The clock read 3:30 PM, and I was still on a call. It pissed me off all the yapping they were doing. I could sense the body temperature rising. They eventually got off the phone 15 minutes later. I shut my station down so fast, waved to Mrs. Bush bye, and I was out of the floor space in 2 minutes. I reached into my locker and got all my belongings. Soon as I got in the car, I put on my Nicki Minaj playlist. I also turned on my GPS to take me to the hotel of my dreams. Even though I drive in the city, I needed directions. I preferred not to cause accidents by turning on one-way streets. I was so excited about driving down that I could not contain myself.

~

IT WAS 6 PM when I hauled into the hotel's parking lot entrance. The valet was there, and he motioned for me to stop. I rolled down the window and asked, "Sir, I am supposed to be meeting my cousin. She a cute redbone and... Up nevermind."

Dani was standing right behind him with a black blouse, blue jeans, and black strapped heels.

"Sir, can you take his keys? He has not had to park his car before. I will help him to his bags and room," she said in a high-pitched voice.

"Yes, ma'am," the valet man responded, "Sir, get all of your belongings, for you won't be coming back until you check out. And welcome to the Four Points by Sheraton at the French Quarter."

I showed a slight smile on my face. My head nodded, and I did what I was told. I grabbed my backpack and my suit-case. I signed the paperwork for the car, and I gave him my keys.

"Now, cousin," Dani spoke with that funny voice again, "Are you happy? This is surprise number 1."

"Cousin, I could cry. I can't believe you got us a room here. We passed by this hotel all the time when walking on Bourbon. This is the shit."

I was so giddy. "And why are you talking like you bougie and ghetto with a twang?"

She pulled down her sunshades, too close to the tip of her nose. "Come, come along, darling."

She tried to sound more British; however, she failed. We both laughed. So we were walking through the hall; I was just taking it all in.

"So AJ," she finally was talking in her normal voice, "we are going to get into this elevator because I already checked us in."

I just shrugged. I was wondering why she was telling me. So she took me where we ended up on the 3rd floor. We walked to this room, where she opened the door with her key.

"Ok, Sir. To the left, we have the bathroom. I love the soap dispensers that are in the shower. Plus, the showerhead can be handheld. Oh, that mirror is nice as well." Dani gave a tour of the room, so giddy. "You have two beds, nice TV, and a dresser table combo. Oh no, didn't I mention two beds? So you can bring someone in here if you'd like."

She playfully pinches me.

"Girl, you know damn well I ain't bring nobody in this room. We both are staying in here." I remarked.

Dani just ignored my statement. She stated, "Let's go outside, shall we." My eyebrows raised like The Rock on WWE.

We walked outside, and my mouth dropped. She had got us a balcony room on the corner. You could catch a splendid view of Toulouse Street and Bourbon Street. People were already out on the street, getting drunk and partying.

"Boy, you better not start crying. Staying here is what you always wanted. You always talked about getting a room— one like this in particular. Now we actually are staying on Bourbon Street. By the way, I bought two rooms. This one is yours."

"That is why I didn't see your stuff. I might bring somebody up here and get a lil' nasty," I said with a cackle so hard I choked.

"See," she said in a giggle. "That is what you get. I am going to my room. Relax a little and settle in here. I'll be back in 45 minutes. So we can start my itinerary."

"Yes, ma'am Boss Lady," I said, hugging her. My smile stretched across my face. She chuckled and left me out on the balcony. I just stood there for 5 minutes, reflecting and viewing the nightlife. I then took a nice shower. So I went to the suitcase. I got my clothes and accessories out. And put them on. I had just finished my hygienic routine when suddenly…

Bang! Bang! I looked through the peephole.

"Ok, Dani, you look damn amazing," I said as I opened the door. "If I wasn't gay?"

"Pause," she said as she grinned. The red wrap front mini dress fit her just right, paired with her black heels. Her fingers did a snap and twirled around. "Number one, you would still be my cousin. We don't do that incest shit ova here. And two, you wouldn't stand a chance. Anyway, you look different. Turn around."

I did a little GQ spin. I was wearing a fresh MJ Bulls jersey, khaki jeans, and Jordan 1 Retros.

"Ok. I see you. I may reconsider."

"Cousin, I wanted to do something different. I want to give Boy."

"You mean you wanted to be Trade. And yes! I am familiar with some of y'all lingo. You ready?"

Oh, my God. My stomach felt like it had stitches ready to pop out; I was laughing so hard. All I could do was nod.

So we caught the elevator and traveled downstairs. We walked through the eloquently designed lobby.

Next thing you know, we were on Bourbon Street. The smell in the air was stale of spilled alcohol and pee. I watched the mounds of people walking and dancing in the street. The sounds of multiple clubs blaring different music are what I loved about this street.

"So Cousin, we are leaving for Cafe Pontalba and then the Cats Meow."

"Ok, cool. Let's put it in the GPS on my phone."

DING! Ding! It was a message from Shamar on HBG.

Hey, I can't meet you tonight, but I got something to do. Can I see you tomorrow?

UGH! I was so pissed. However, I played it cool and messaged him back for sure.

"Trouble with a homie?" Dani asked.

"Nah, I will just meet up with him tomorrow."

"It's ok, AJ."

We began following the GPS directions to the cafe. Not that far. It only took us about 8 minutes to get there walking. It looked very nice. We sat at a table, and a friendly server about my size and height came over. She was a lovely bleach blonde with a soft voice. As she took our orders, I got nervous. I wished to tell Dani about my status. Now was a good time. I ordered the spicy cajun shrimp, and Dani ordered the calamari.

"So Dani. I need to tell you something important." My mind was racing as I gulped because I was so nervous. My fingers were twitching.

"What's up, Cousin? This sounds really serious."

"Well. It is about my rape."

"Ok, let me prepare myself more. What else could happen or go wrong?" Dani started rambling on about Jim and Melissa. How much she hated the situation. I had to stop her. Before I could say anything, the server brought us our food.

"Dani. I'm HIV positive." I said it loud enough to where she could hear me.

Dani stared at me sadly for 2 seconds. Then she grabbed her fork and plucked off one of my shrimp. She shrugged, "Ok."

Her response puzzled me. "Ok?"

"Cousin, listen. I love you. I would never turn my back on you. My friend, Lisa, needed help to study one night for a test. The subject was infectious diseases. I learned so much. Still going to drink after you. Still going to pick food off of your plate. You can't give it to me. Unless you are not on meds." She pointed her fork at me. "You are taking your meds and consistently, right?"

"Yes, cousin. I am. But don't tell Terrence and Jackson."

"I won't. Well, I guess Tee Joanne and Momo Jean knew. I doubt if Melissa knows? Yet, I wonder if she has it?"

"That is a good question. Maybe he told her. Thank you for being there for me."

"Of course. That is what cousins are for."

She picked off another shrimp off my plate. I just grinned from ear to ear. Our food was light, and we delighted in its taste. We were aware we were going to go to our favorite pizza spot later. We paid and left the server a $6 tip.

As we were leaving, we realized we were right next to Jackson Square. We noticed so many tarot card readers and palm readers.

"Aiden, one of us should do it," expressed Dani.

"I don't think we should have this experience. The church always taught us not to mess with that," I said, concerned.

We were moving away from the front of the cafe. I overheard footsteps behind us. We turned around; however, nobody was there.

"I am here," she purred.

We whipped our heads back forward. A beautiful woman stood looking to be of creole descent. She looked to be in her late 30s or early 40s. She was standing about 5 feet 9 inches, wearing a red turban on her head. The half-white shirt she wore had a galactic black hole design on it. Her skirt was hues of red, orange, and yellow draping down to her ankles, where she wore some brown sandals.

"I have a word for you, young man. Usually, people pay for my services, but something led you here, my son. Come, take a seat at my table."

"I am sorry, ma'am, but…"

"Oh, young mister, you are Aiden Josiah, son of Joanne and the grandson David and Jean Phillips. You should come and sit down."

It surprised me how she knew that. Dani said with a murmur in my ear, "How does she know our people?"

"Sure, I will sit down with you." She intrigued me by who she was. She looked familiar, but I just could not place her.

So we followed the woman to her table in Jackson Square. Not that far. I came and sat down. Dani stood up behind me.

She shuffled her cards. "Hello you two, I am Angèle Breaux, and I read palms, and I do tarot card readings. I also am clairvoyant and clairaudient, so I can see and hear your loved ones who have passed," Angèle gave us her spill.

"Before we begin, let me ask you this," I asked. I want some insight into what her answer would be. "Are you related to the Breaux out in Marais Vert?"

She looked at me and winked. I politely got up. "Thank you for your interest, ma'am, but I cannot entertain this."

Dani pushed me down in the chair. She said in a whisper, "Take it as a grain of salt. Let's hear what she says." Then in her regular voice to Angèle, "Ma'am, please continue."

"Thank you, sweetie," she replied, "But, I cannot continue unless the person who I have a message for saying it's ok."

"Fine." I was getting annoyed. "Please tell me."

She held my hand and hummed. Her actions were making me anxious. She then took out her cards. The explanation she gave us was there are many tarots and oracle decks. She wanted to use The Starter Tarot, The New Orleans Voodoo Tarot, The Moon Oracle Deck, and The Romance Angels Oracle Deck.

"That is a lot of different decks," I said in a low mutter.

"Well," Angèle replied. "That is because I use each deck for different things. So when I explain what's happening, you have a clear understanding."

I knew if I had said something else smart, I would have annoyed her. I just wanted this reading over. For Dani's sake, I continued with it. I kept thinking hard that I needed to relax because she might read my thoughts.

"Ah, yes," Angèle spoke as she was flipping cards, "if you think too hard, I can read minds too."

I took my hand and hit my head like Homer Simpson. I just breathed and tried to clear out my mind.

"Ok, I am done," she smiled, "I am ready to explain what is happening with you."

I rolled my eyes, "I am totally ready now."

"Hmm," Angèle stated, "okey-doke."

She took a deep breath. Each deck she had out had a different amount of cards to them.

"This is The Starter Tarot deck. I used this deck because this seems to be your first reading ever. These cards explain and have written explanations on them to help you. Now I like to do a seven-card spread. It has two rows, three columns, and one last card on the end. Aiden, a lot was going on. Or is going on with you, rather. I had four more cards to pull up. So this is what I am seeing. The first card pulled is the knight of coins. This represents the person you are. You are a mature person who is dependable and works hard. But, I see a deep sadness." She looks at us as we are getting emotional. I put my head down. She then closes her eyes. "Actually, the word I just heard for both of you was Momo. You both are grieving. She is informing me she was with PawPaw. She is a kind of soft speaker. But I see her with what appears to be her husband and son. They are all well."

"Oh my God," Dani burst into tears as she is rubbing my shoulders. I silently cry.

Angèle carried on to say, "This grief you feel correlates with your second card. That is nine of swords. Despair and sleeplessness can wear you down. Plus, you, Aiden, have another issue that weighs heavy on you. That deals with your 3rd and 4th cards. They feel like a couple to me. The man is the magician with your 3rd card. He is best at deceiving your family and perhaps his wife. His wife is the 4th card, the queen of wands. This card is in the reverse position. It means there is jealousy and opposition on her part."

"Ok, I definitely believe this can't be fake because how in…"

"Shush, Aiden. I'm sorry, Momo has tears. She said that she is sorry. Another young man is stepping forward; however, I cannot make it out. It's like he is alive, but he is deceased. But Momo keeps repeating how sorry she was and how they made the wrong decision."

I released a flood of tears because she hit the nail on the head with Melissa and Jim. Dani rubbed my back and leaned over and hugged me.

"Aiden, do not let your grief and this situation deter you. Sometimes family and others will try to discourage you. It is going to be hard. Though, this magician has more dark secrets. Whoa. More than you can ever imagine. But, he somehow will get what he deserves. You will gain strength, and justice will happen. The strength card is your 6th card, and justice is the last card of your main spread."

"Wow." It amazed and intrigued me at the same time. "Ok. What are those four cards?"

"Why are there two young male energies in the spread? They keep popping up. There is a connection with them. They will try to help you somehow. These young men associate with one another. I cannot pinpoint their connection," she stated.

I was thinking maybe that, nope. It couldn't be.

"So I pulled a page of wands, which is the first person. He has information and is consistent. He might even facilitate you to meet someone close to him. This is where the 4 of cups card comes into play. This person you will meet will have a king of swords' energy. Very determined and ambitious. I see a romance if you take it there. Ultimately, this is a lifelong friendship. It symbolizes this in the Lovers' card."

I quietly let out a snicker to myself. I thought of 2 people. But I could not picture them knowing each other.

"So continuing, the Moon Oracle cards you have in your top 3 are the guru, first-quarter waxing earth-moon equaling stability, and the wedding. The guru represents you in how you are trying to escape something. Someone will come along and offer you stability. Also, notice that these first two cards deal with your sun and moon signs, Pisces and Virgo, respectively. The marriage card is about following socially acceptable norms; you two will struggle in this area. However, your bottom three cards are Venus, gibbous waxing water moon equaling passion, and full water moon equaling fulfillment. This entails you, and this person has come up with a creative, unique approach. It will lead to clarity and fulfillment."

"It's a lot to think about," I stated. I was taking heed of the messages that were coming through.

"Finally, your Romantic Angels' oracle cards, in order are you deserve love, let your friends help you, and chemistry. Empathize with yourself that someone will love me. Seek help from this lovely lady sitting by you and others. Someone around the corner for you to get reacquainted with. Please believe that."

"Wow, thank you for doing this for him. It was discerning for both of us," Dani said as her interpretation.

"There is no need to thank me," Angèle had shown her lovely smile. "I am just a messenger. We will re-encounter each other."

She winked at me. I got up and thanked her for everything.

"You know that was rather spirited, Dani. I have to admit to believing in stuff like that." I said to clarify as we walked up the corner.

She paused, "Yeah. I know. You always watched Celebrity Ghost Stories on A&E. But, you noticed she never went over the New Orleans Voodoo Tarot with you."

"Really?!"

"Yes! Let's go back."

We traveled back to the spot where we had the reading. She and her table had vanished. It's like they were never there. I started scratching my head. Dani gasped because this stunned us. We wanted to ask people, but we feared their responses.

"Ok, this is weird. Let's just have fun on Bourbon."

"Yeah, Dani. Let us go."

Man, this was crazy. We got to the corner. I felt like eyes were watching me. I shrugged it off and was ready for some fun.

7

CLUBBIN' ON BOURBON & AN OLD ACQUAINTANCE

Trying to shake off what happened, Dani and I strutted up two blocks on Saint Peter Street. We were laughing and talking about where we headed. We got to the intersection of Saint Peter and Bourbon. The "Cats Meow" sign glowed so vibrantly in neon green and pink.

"We are here. Did you look up the karaoke list already?" Dani was excited. I was too. I loved doing karaoke, especially at Philly's, my favorite club back home in Marais Vert.

"Girl, yes. I don't know the song I want to do. There's so much music on their list."

"I think I'm gonna do a rock song." Dani plays air guitar.

"Guh, No ma'am," I said with a roaring laugh. People started looking in my direction because of how funny my laugh sounded.

"Ugh! What?! I am trying to get my HER on," She said with a light chuckle.

"Come on."

So as we are crossing the street, I heard somebody singing "Bootylicious" by Destiny's Child.

It can't be. We looked at each other, thinking we recognized someone's voice.

We continued through the crowd. Entering the club, we stood at the back. It who we thought it was. Indigo.

She was wearing a red body con mini dress that had one shoulder with a red strappy heel. She styled her hair with two braids in the front, going to a sleek, curly ponytail. By this time, she ended her song. We had moved up to the stage.

"Hey. It's funny I came across you guys here. Did you like the performance?" Indigo had put on the fakest smile.

"Yeah, you sounded good," I said. She was already faking. I tried to be genuine with her.

"Thanks." She curtsied and waved as if everybody was looking at her. "So, did you plan on meeting us up here or matching us? I think it's a little stalker-ish. You know?"

Dani got annoyed, "Indi, what are you talking about?"

"You're about to see now. Babe! Look what the cat drug into meow?" She said sarcastically.

Jevaun exited the bathroom. When I saw him, my heart started fluttering. He started walking towards us with a Pippen Bulls and khaki jeans similar to mine. Not only that, he had on the Jordan 13 Bred sneakers. Their colors were red and black.

"What up, Little Homie," Jay gave me dap, "Daniiiii." He hugged her. "Are we double dating or something?" He acted way more excited to see us. That materialized a welcoming emotion. "AJ, I guess we a team. Lead me to the ship."

He held out his hand up top for the high five. I obliged him.

"So, did you sing yet?" I asked him.

"Nope, I wasn't planning on it. But since you're here, I will work up the nerve."

Indigo stood right there, feeling ignored. "Uh, I am standing right here, jerk."

He gave her a look that could cut through glass. It seems like she wanted to continue having a pleasant evening, so she stopped complaining.

"Y'all, she knows I sing with her all the time. So, Dani, I think you should sing first. Then, Aiden and I will go. Cool?"

Dani looked at Indi. "Cool. Let's go sign up."

As they walked away, Indigo eyed me up and down.

"I guess he interested in both of you."

"Girl, what?!" I could not take her seriously. "Indigo, you are a beautiful girl, and y'all make an attractive couple. Girl, what gives?"

"Maybe it has something to do with his brother's passing. I had all his attention. Well, between me and his mom, of course. He never really showed interest in having other friends or people in his life." She shushed me. "Here they come. We never had this conversation. Comprende?"

With a soft chuckle, I said, "What conversation? We wanted to know both of you."

She smiled a bit. God knows I did not lie when I said that. There was one truth that remained. I had a little crush on Jay. Plus, I still conversed with Shamar. I decided to message him on the app.

Wish you were here.

The host got on stage. The crowd continued to leave in and out of the Cat's Meow.

"Now," the host stated in his deep baritone voice. He announced her as if it a stadium full of people who attended. "Give it up for Dani. She will perform 'What's Love Got To Do With It' by Tina Turner."

I screamed as the crowd cheered. She put her hand up to her head in shame. She started singing the song low. But by the time it was the second verse, she was dancing like Miss Turner from her Live in Rio 88 concert. Everybody started singing the song with her and clapping. When the song was over, she received a warmer round of applause.

The host came back to the stage. "Now that was great. Give it up again for Miss Dani." The crowd cheered again. "Now I got told this duo is going to sing a classic NSYNC song, Bye Bye Bye. Welcome to the Cats Meow stage, Jay and AJ."

I looked at him like you cannot be serious. He laughed, patted me on my head, and gave me the follow him symbol with his hand. The host gave us the mics. Before the song started, Jay looked up the lyrics. He said in a murmur, "I'm JT and you JC."

I had to let that laugh out loud before the song started. So, I started since JC's verse positioned first. Nervousness had set in. I pretended to be back at home in Philly's. My voice grew in confidence. Jay sang his parts well. The most fun everyone had was when we harmonized together. We even copied the choreography from the video. People came off of Bourbon Street to peep their heads in on our performance. When we ended the song, the place became packed. We bowed and got off the stage.

"Say we did it," Jay remarked, "proud of you, man."

"Thanks."

The girls came over to our location in the club.

"Y'all really did well," Indi said in a jealous tone.

Dani looked at her like, can you put a damn smile on your face? Then she hugged me and gave Jay a hi-five. So all four of us walked out of the club.

Jay put me in a playful headlock. "Man, I did not know you could blow somewhat." He gave me a noogie.

Indi acted annoyed to where she cleared her throat. She whined, "Jay, can we end the night early? I wanna go back to the hotel."

"Give us one second," He said to Dani and me.

They moved out of our viewpoint. The crowds traveled different ways along the street. The music from multiple clubs played loud to where we couldn't listen to their discussion. We only could see gestures. When they walked back towards us, I could tell who won the argument.

"Dani, Aiden. I'm down for turning up. But, she wants to go back to the Four Points," Jay said solemnly.

"Uh, that's where we are staying," Dani said in a mumble. I chuckled. The stare on Indi's face was priceless. It came across like, damn, how can I get rid of y'all. She perceived defeat.

"You know what? I am just going to hang. I have really been a bitch. You guys haven't deserved it. I am sorry," Indigo with a sigh. "I guess I am a little…"

"Selfish." I made the duck face with my lips.

"Self-centered." Dani crossed her arms.

"Bossy!" Jay tilted his head to the side.

"Ummm...," Indi considering herself attacked, "Bratty."

"Ohhhhhh." We had to laugh at our simultaneous reaction.

"So let's just turn up, you guys. What's next?"

It disappointed her a tad bit. I caught it in her voice.

But I was determined not to let her bring down my spirits. My cousin paid for me to come and party. I was going to do that.

"So, I am thinking we go get hand grenades from Tropical Isle. We hit one bar. Then we eat pizza at Vieux Carre. We can bar hop some more. Then repeat."

Dani gave a small smile. I waited, hoping for some push back.

"Well, I'm down," Jay said as his answer. "Indi?"

He had put the pressure on her. We all looked at her with intent. She paused with a lot of dramatics. "Let's do it."

Laughing loud must be a Phillips' trait. Dani surprised even me with her laugh. Everyone who was walking around us happened to look crazy at her when she laughed. "Cousin, let's roll on these streets."

So it was still early for Bourbon street. It occurred around 9:30, and the crowds had grown. We crossed over the road. We passed by the cops on their horses, little hot dog stands, and dodged the puddles of spilled liquor and urine. When we got to Tropical Isle's Bayou Club, it is customary that they ID you before entering. We entered and ordered our style of the hand grenade. The hand grenade is Tropical Isle's signature liquid concoction. You order the daiquiris either on the rocks or frozen. The girls got theirs on the rocks while we got ours frozen.

We stayed there dancing, sipping on our drinks, and getting to know each other. Dani and I learned so much about Indigo and Jevaun, including how they met. Indi did most of the explaining.

Indigo Musa graduated from Loyola University with her Bachelor of Business Administration in International Business with a minor in Women's Studies. She plans to build centers in the US and Nigeria to help girls like her become more invested in entrepreneurship.

Now, Jevaun Black graduated from Tulane University with his Bachelors of Science in Management with an entrepreneurship specialization and a minor in Music Science and Technology. He wanted to manage artists in music someday.

They met growing up in New Orleans. They have always had friends since 5th grade. His mother, Alvita, loved her.

Both of them worked at a Verizon call center. By the time Indigo finished talking, it was 10:45, and we had finished our drinks.

"We are taking over the world," Indi stated. Jay looked at her, giving her a slight nod of the head.

"So, y'all, let's go to Razzoo's," I stated excitedly.

SO WE THREW AWAY our cups, and we walked down the street. Long lines came out of both doors.

Razzoo's attendance packed it out. We had a system where we all held hands. We got through the crowd, finding a spot. The bar stayed as full as the dance floor. Up at the front, women of all backgrounds and colors were flashing their boobs. All we did was laugh. The music was a mix of 90s hip hop, today's pop and rap charts, and reggaeton. The MC had a guy come upon the stage; he blindfolded him. So then he picked people from the crowd: 3 girls and a guy. So the contest was a lap dance. I fell out laughing at all the contestants. It was all in good fun. The person receiving the lap dances laughed off all of them.

"Woah, that's my song." I danced. Jay was holding Indi but was facing us on this cramped dance floor. The club blared "All Eyes on You". Even with people around, I could overhear Jay rapping Meek verse to Indi. But when Nicki's verse came on, I rhymed it like I always do. However, I could tell he was continuing to pay attention to me. Then they started playing everything. People were jumping too close to me. I was trying to make room to watch others dance.

"Cousin, you smell that?" Dani asked me. Hell, I checked under my damn armpits. Then Indi and Jay's faces scrounged up. "Oh, hell no! a new club, please."

We lined up together and followed each other out.

"Y'all not hungry?"

"Yeah, cousin. I don't know if they have been to Vieux Carre," I responded. "We should go, though."

"We usually go to the other ones. But we can try this one," Jay said. Indi nodded.

So WE MADE our way up the street to Vieux Carre Pizza. While we stood in line, Indi and Jay asked us what the best pizza was.

"Well, I always get their all meats pizza." I was licking my lips as we were getting closer to the cash register.

Jay snickered, "I should have known you were going to get pizza loaded with meat."

I hit my hand on my head and chuckled. Indigo just looked at him. Dani cracked up laughing. We ordered the all meats pizza. Jay finished his pizza before I finished mine.

"So I see there are no complaints," I smarted off. We all laughed.

Indi wondered, "Didn't you say we were going to The Swamp?"

"Yeah, let's go. I wanna ride that thang," Dani smirked.

Jay made a face, and Indi punched him lightly on the arm.

So we walked over to The Swamp. Before we walked to the back patio, we patronized the bar and got shots. We arrived; the line was not long. There was a tall, gorgeous black beauty on the bull. She tries to hold on for dear life. She fell off after 5 seconds.

"Fuck it," she screamed. She snatched her lace front off her head and started swinging it around. She stayed on the bull for 20 seconds that next time.

We were all cracking up. The whole outside part was in an uproar of laughter. And then it was my turn to go next. Luckily, I had 5 dollars in my pocket, stashed away. I gave it to the bull operator. I got on, twisting the rope around my right hand. The crew was looking at me. I knew I was trying to impress them.

The bull started turning this way, that way, and vibrated. That is when I bit my lip. It whipped around. I looked over to see everyone was cheering me on. I finally fell off after 25 seconds.

Indi was after me and let's say she tried oozing sex appeal all over the bull. She had given Dani her phone to take good shots and video. When she finished and got her phone back, she hugged Dani. It shocked me.

"So you not going to ride, Dani?" Indi asked.

Dani said, cracking up, "Oh no, ma'am, you did enough riding for me."

I wanted to laugh so badly at her shady comment. My hands covered my mouth. Indi thought nothing of it.

"Girl, I love these pics. Babe, she did good, huh?" Indi stated as she handed him the phone. He looked, nodded, and grabbed her by her waist.

I was a little jealous. So I got my phone, and I messaged Shamar.

Hey, I know it's late but could you come to Bourbon Street. Message me, please.

So I put my phone down. We all decided next to the little Tropical Isle up the street. We passed through, getting another round of hand grenades. So when we came out, one bar started playing "The Cupid Shuffle". It was loud enough for people walking down the street to overhear. By this time, I had finished my second-hand grenade fast. So I was dancing, and this girl steps on my foot.

"Uh, excuse me?" I slurred.

"So what I stepped on your foot. Johnny!" she said, flipping her blonde hair.

Here steps this six foot one man that wants to stand in my face. "So what you said to my girl, you little fag?"

They gave the statement, and I was clueless about why. I stood there looking in a daze. But when I blinked twice, Jevaun was standing in front of Indi and Dani, who was standing by me.

"Mon luk. Yuh gyal did wrang. Step tuh him an wi will hab problem dem. Yuh feel me?" Jay asserted.

The guy and his girl walked away. I blinked, thinking I saw Angèle. I couldn't move because I was in shock. Did she see the whole thing? Was she following me?

Jay turned around to everyone, asking me was I ok. I was fine, but I still wanted to party. We advanced to Funky 544, a bar right across the street from the hotel. It was around 2 AM. We continued in the club. The music was R&B and hip hop. I proceeded to the bar for another drink. "Can We Talk" sounded through the club. I joined the people, and the entire club was singing it. So some guys came. One was cute. He started flirting with me, and we danced a little. So I was becoming into him and flirting. I looked out the door; she was there. Angèle lingered in the street. I perceived she was coming into the club. She wasn't there when I blinked. I thought to myself, I better end the dance with this guy. Although he seemed handsome, I got freaked out after I saw Angèle.

Tiredness befell my body. I knew what that meant. I needed to get to my room before I crash. It neared 3:30 in the morning, and my eyes endured heaviness.

"Hey y'all, I am about to turn in. I had fun," I sounded so tired to myself.

"Aww, Now I wanna party some more," Indi whined.

Jay thought of a solution. "Listen, I am going up with him. I gotta make sure he is straight and then prepare the room for you."

Indi looked deep into his eyes and kissed him.

"I would say y'all get a room. Oops, too late. Y'all got one." Dani had to poke fun at them.

"COUSIN, YOU OK?"

I tried to make a serious face. I wasn't conscious of the effects of all the alcohol I drank. "Yeah, Dani. Thank you for everything. See you in the morning. And you too. Don't worry, and I got it. I had fun tonight."

I started walking out the door. My feet stumbled a bit when stepping out. People persisted in partying. They were walking in every which direction. Once I was at the hotel door, I detected a tap on my shoulder. It was Jay.

"Man, I told you I was coming to make sure you straight. Mon yuh eaise haad," Jay with a groan.

I chuckled as we carried on to the hallway into the elevator.

"Man, I can feel my face," I slurred, "I am sleepy. 3rd floor, please."

Jay just shook his head. I leaned against the wall of the elevator.

"We here, man. So where is your room?"

I slept in the corner. He open slapped my arm, and I jumped.

"Man, what are you doing?"

"Come on, man. Where the room?"

"It's at the end of the hall."

"Bruh, grab my neck. Wrap your legs around like I'm your brother or something."

"I am not that color." I got big-eyed. Those words I had spoken were inner thoughts. I couldn't believe I said that. I started laughing aloud. My pointer finger went over my mouth to hush me. I didn't want to antagonize the guests who were sleeping with my noisiness.

"See, you got a..." He knew I was drunk. But he also caught that shade I threw at Indi.

He shook his head, put my arm over his, and helps me to walk to my room. I barely was any help. I gave him the key, and he somehow opens the door. He dropped me on the first bed. My eyes were half-open, and I experienced dizziness. Suddenly, I was having a warm sensation like someone was holding me just for a bit. He got off the bed. Then Jevaun kneeled right next to my face.

"Mi lakka yuh mon. Mi wish deh did ah way." Jay said in a whisper.

My eyes were so groggy, still barely able to open them. So I opened them halfway. I said the name of who I thought I saw. "Goodnight, Shamar."

It had taken him aback by what I said. He wanted to wake me up and question why I said Shamar's name. However, he didn't. He left and went up to his room to prepare it for his girlfriend. His mind still wondered as I was fast asleep in my room.

8

A HANGOVER, IT'S ALRIGHT, & DISAPPOINTMENT

I woke up to "We Are Family" playing on my phone and the banging on my hotel door. It was 8 AM, and my head was thumping.

"I'm coming!" I said in a yell. Ugh, I must have drunk too much. I meandered to open the door.

Dani wore a comfortable gray Adidas tracksuit and gray sneakers. "Boy. We supposed to get to Café du Monde before we go to church. You ain't even dressed yet."

She sits on the bed closest to the balcony door. She had a water bottle in her hand. I was holding my head as she was talking to me.

"What happened last night with Jay, Aiden Josiah?" She asked me in a stern voice. "Indigo called me this morning. She said she enjoyed us, and her night ended lovely. But, Jay acts frigid to her if she mentions you."

"Dani, I don't remember. I'm aware he helped me in the room." My hands held my pounding head. "I'm really sorry."

"Here, drink this." She hands me the water bottle. "You already aware I came prepared."

"Thanks. He helped me in the room; I was in and out." I pondered as I drank. "But the weird thing is, I thought I saw my friend in my room. You are familiar with Mr. HBG. I don't understand. He left his number, though, so we could keep in contact."

"Well, text him. Indigo, when her guard is low, she a pretty chill girl. So you got 40 minutes, mister, because ah we going to Café du Monde and church."

"Ok."

She leaves my room so I can get ready. I was still wondering what I had said to Jay. So I texted him.

Hey, man! It's Aiden. Thanks for helping me last night. I had loads of fun last night hanging with you and Indigo. Sorry for getting so drunk. I have a killer headache. KIT man.

So I got myself showered up and put my clothes on. I went knocked on Dani's room door.

"Humph. You look cute," She smirked.

I had on a pink tie-dye shirt and blue jeans from American Eagle with the John Wall cherry blossom sneakers.

"Thanks, you ready?"

"Yep."

So we left the hotel and walked to Café du Monde. We arrived at the restaurant, viewing no long lines. We could get our beignets and go. Dani was skipping back to the hotel like a big kid. The beignets covered her face with a powdery sweetness. All I could do was laugh.

I didn't want to leave the hotel when we got there. We made our way to our rooms and packed up to check out. I changed into my navy blue suit, white dress shirt, and tan dress shoes by Kenneth Cole. I met Dani down in the lobby area, where she was already checking us out. She was wearing a faux two-piece navy blue floral print dress with navy blue peep-toe heels.

"Come on now." She said. She had a sunny disposition with a sigh and a chuckle. "You had to go in my suitcase. This doesn't make no sense."

"Well, we a family unit. We just have great minds and ok style."

She puts her hand on her hip. "Yeah, speak for yourself. I have great impeccable style."

"My, my. Such big words."

She playfully hits me on the arm.

"Ow."

We grabbed our luggage and got into our cars. Traffic was not that bad. We made it to church 10 minutes early.

The praise and worship was moving. However, nothing was more touching than Bianca McKee, the pastor's daughter, singing her rendition of "Everything Will Be Alright" by Isaiah Templeton. You could sense every note in her voice as her brother, Doc, played the piano. She sang it with such grace and feeling.

Her solo was the perfect opening for her father's message for today. The sermon was "In Our Suffering: He is Here". Pastor McKee had us shedding tears as he gave us scriptures passages of Proverbs 3: 5 - 6 and James 1: 2 - 4. He explained how those scriptures got him through the hurts, pains, and darkness in his life. The thing he relayed to us was when he talked about his grief over his mother. We left out of the church. We detected more strengthened by the word we had just heard.

I FOLLOWED her to Momo Jean's house after church. When we pulled, I saw a short, dreaded dark complexed man sitting on the steps. There is only one person who wears cut up jeans, a torn tee, and Chuck Taylor shoes. That was my cousin, Jacob. He was sitting on the porch waiting for Terrence to give him some weed like he always does.

"Hey, Dani," he spoke to her and not me.

I did nothing to him, but he is both of sisters' keeper. I stopped and spoke, anyway.

"Hey, Jacob. Uh, how is it going?" I asked.

"You alright, bruh."

"Aha. Well, excuse me. I'm tryna get into Momo's house. Can you push over?"

"Say one more and..." Jacob stood up tall at 5'9" on the steps. He has his fist clenched. Scruffy, facial hair ravaged his face.

"And what?!" Terrence came out of the house, overhearing our exchange. "And what?"

Jacob sat back down.

"Aiden, you straight?" Terrence asked me.

"Yeah, I was tryna be a friendly cousin. He just doesn't like me. I'm going into the house."

I journeyed inside. Dani and Terrence stayed out on the porch with Jacob. Jackson was sitting there watching TV and shaking his head.

"Come on, man. The game is about to start."

"Yep. The Patriots are going make sushi out the Dolphins," I stated.

I appreciated the guy's time with Jackson and Terrence. There is a misconception I always felt. Feminine gay guys, like me, don't know about sports. I recognize a little about penalty rules, positions, offense, defense, and even football and basketball terminology. So I admired the fact that I could be myself and hang with them. They loved me and never judged me.

"No, don't hit him, T," I listened to Dani holler at Terrence from outside.

Jackson shook his head. "Cuz, don't worry about it. He is tripping over you with jealousy."

"Yeah, Cuz. I know."

They came into the house. Terrence moved into the kitchen while Dani sat next to me.

"AJ," Dani smirked, "that cousin of ours. He got a vendetta against you for no reason. Other than you and Melissa not getting along. Well, that and Uncle John's ways about gay people."

Uncle John is Regina, Melissa, and Jacob's father. He hadn't spoken to my mom or me except for Momo Jean's funeral. As always, I tried to be nice, but after my mom heard him talking about me, she told me not to worry about him. He and Regina traveled back to Houston, Texas, without saying bye to anyone but Melissa and Jacob.

I had to breathe out. "Yeah, Dani. I noticed."

Terrence stood in the kitchen doorway. "I know if you don't pop that nigga, I'm gonna do it. Real Shit. Don't let him punk you or take your kindness for weakness."

I nodded my head, yes. I realized he meant I have to stand up for myself a tad more.

Terrence had finished cooking by the time of the Saints versus the Rams game. I was feeling my stomach up with steak, baked beans, corn, and mashed potatoes. Man, we were watching the game and yelling at that TV. It disgusted us how our home team was playing. The Saints ended up losing 9 to 24.

DING! Ding!

I got a notification on HBG. It was Shamar.

Hey, I'm sorry I couldn't come to Bourbon but meet me on the lakefront later.

I messaged him back.

Text you when I finished spending time with my family. Is that ok?

He sent a smiley face, so I knew he was ok with it.

"Mm-hmm," Dani gave me a shady look.

"What is that for?"

"You better watch the reunion show with me before you go."

Terrence butted in the discourse. "I'll watch the reunion show with you. I think Candiace is pretty cute."

Each looked at each other puzzled.

"What?! Y'all don't tease me because I'm a hard nigga that watches housewives. Plus, Evette put me on. Ya know."

"Aha. All for Evette," Jackson stated, "You really like this chick, huh?"

Big T blushed.

"Aww, cousin," Dani said with a giggle, "I know you."

He throws a couch pillow at her. "Stop y'all."

So we all ended up watching The Real Housewives of Potomac reunion. Then I told them goodbye and that I would see them later.

So I DROVE to the lakefront. I parked in my usual spot.

Tap. Tap.

I rolled the window down, and there he was. He was just as handsome as when we first met. I got a nagging suspicion something was wrong. He was wearing the same outfit he wore when he saw me last. I'm not one to judge anybody; I placed it in the back of my mind.

"Unlock di door, please," he said.

I couldn't contain my excitement. I was excited to see him. So I hit the button and let him in.

"Hey," I said in a shy voice. "What's been up with you? Why haven't I seen you?"

"Listen, Mi hab bin real busy," he stated, "Mi ave sum bad news. Mia a move aweh."

"I just started trying to get to know you. This sucks. But where are you going? At least we have the app."

"Yuh a amazing. Nuh figet ih. Buh mi nuh waan tuh bi tied dung tuh nutten. I hope you understand we should just be friends. I want to be clear with you."

"That's fine. Um… Can I message you later? I gotta get home."

"Mi hush. Call If you need someone to talk to. I will be here. I promise."

I made light of it. "Yeah. I bet."

He apologized again as he exited the car. I wasn't listening. I started liking someone, and this happens. It was like, what is the point. I told him bye and drove off. Listening to heartbreaking songs on the way home was feeding my feelings. I was so disappointed. I got home around 11:30.

"So you're home early," My mom said soon as I walked in the door.

I said nothing. My steps quickened to my room and closed the door. I sobbed a little and wanted to message him on HBG, but I decided against it. I felt like such a loser. But this was the beginning of my downward spiral.

9

THE ACCIDENT, THE PARTY TIME SETUP & UTTER DEPRESSING CHAOS

As the weeks passed by, I tried to forget about Shamar. I would message him to see if I would get a response. Of course, I wouldn't get one.

Also, adding to my failures is my keeping contact with Jevaun. We had texted; in fact, I started texting both Indigo and Jevaun. I would sense jealousy from Indigo when texting them both. I had vibes with them both. It's hard for me to make friends. I always stuck up under my family. It was refreshing for me to talk to them. I just stopped talking to both.

It is Friday, the day before Regina's party. I got up super late, so I was rushing.

"Aiden, take your medicine bottle with you. You don't need to forget," Joanne said.

"Yes, mother." I rolled my eyes playfully where she perceived I wasn't disrespectful.

"I saw that."

All I could do was chuckle. I talk to my mom about everything. Well, almost everything. She has been my biggest support besides Dani, Jackson, and Terrence. They have been helping me get through my grief. Through my thoughts, I continued to pack because I would stay the weekend at Momo Jean's house.

I looked. It was 8:00. I needed to be out of the house about 15 minutes ago. My nervousness was getting the better of me. I was running back and forth outside to the car, making sure I had everything. The medicine bottle rattled as an alarm.

"Like I said." My mom rattled the bottle some more. "Do not forget your medicine."

I took it and nodded my head. I traveled in the car and started my commute.

"That child of mine. Keep him, Lord." My mom prayed as she watched me leave from the window.

Traffic was horrible enough for me to call my job. I explained I would be tardy. Tardies are something I hate getting. But I hate getting points more. I arrived at work at 9:10. I was running to my locker. My hands chucked my pill bottle and phone in there once I opened it. I was so clumsy that I spilled pills in my locker. I locked up my locker, thinking that all the medicines were in there. The tardy was what I got when I clocked in. Mrs. Bush stopped me.

"Is everything ok?" Mrs. Bush asked.

"Yes, ma'am. I was just running a little late. The traffic held me up a bit. I appreciate you asking."

She gave a smile. I moved to my seat. I presumed it sincere that my supervisor wanted to keep her employees happy. She was my supervisor, but an expert judge of character and work ethic. She gives people chance after chance on the job. When they self-destruct on the job, that is their cross to bear. That is when I heard Mrs. Bush talking to Glenn about his continued tardiness when I was walking to my seat.

As he was going to his seat, he said with a contemptuous smile, "You a sick girl."

He said it so arrogant and nasty. I wanted to turn around and ask what nonsense he was speaking. The call I was on kept me from doing that. The calls were steadily coming, but that didn't bother me. I continued working until I got a break message. I made my way to my locker and tidied it. Then I came and sat down. I saw Eliza and Bonita.

"Hey y'all," I said with a grin.

Bonita waved, and Eliza just had her head down. She did not even look my way. I found it odd.

"Um. Hey Eliza."

She looked up and gave a quick wave. She sat on the other edge of the table; Bonita sat opposite of me in front of me.

"How have you been?" she asked me.

"I am ok. But what's wrong with her?" I asked.

"I speak for myself. Hmm, let me ponder quickly. I want to know why you didn't tell me you were diseased?" she smarted off.

I gasped, and I was so taken aback.

"Eliza!" Bonita agonized.

"What?! He could have told me. I would not have been that close to him," she remarked.

"Wow. Um..." I was struggling for the words to say. "I thought we were friends. Yes, I am positive. Um, I don't speak about it for reasons like this, anyway. But thanks." I got up and walked back to the call floor.

Bonita called out as I was walking, "Hey, you are still you. It doesn't matter. When you are ready to talk, we can."

"Thanks," I said as an answer. I turned around to give a small twinkle through my sadness. Just then, I got a message from an unknown number. It was a video clip of a musical artist being nasty. The text sent to me along with it was evil.

So you dropped your little pill. Stay alive.

I was familiar with who it was. It made me aware of how they could send me that text. But, I also realized that my mistake. I could have found all my medication had I checked the room. My mind was not on seeing if any pills hit the ground. I put my phone up with a quickness. I needed to go to the bathroom and exit to the call floor. Some of my co-workers were staring at me. They scooted their chairs in further to let me pass. As I sat in my cubicle working, thoughts of Glenn passing around the word that I had HIV came to my head. I tried not to let it bother me.

Lunchtime came, and I clocked out. I rushed to my locker and got my phone. I messaged Dani that it was an emergency. Shamar received a message, too. He said he would be there if I needed him.

I was the first person to take lunch today. So I got my lunch out of the refrigerator. Glenn came out, and he looked at me and laughed. He was now getting under my skin. I wanted to knock him out. But my job was more important than retaliation. So while I am eating, he washes his hands, gets disinfectant spray out of the cabinet, and sprays the refrigerator handle.

Bonita and Eliza came out after us.

"Thanks, Glenn. I don't do germs," Eliza huffed.

Bonita just shook her head.

Eliza amazed me. I thought about people turning on you. Mistreatment was something I would not subject myself to anymore. I finished my lunch and departed back to the call floor.

I focused on my work for the rest of my workday. Co-workers stopped looking at me as Aiden. So, I tried to avoid people as best as I could. Their perception of what I have is all they saw.

Ten minutes before my shift ended, Ms. Bush sent me a supervisor message. I reached her desk, and she instructed me to go to a private meeting room.

"Aiden, I just want you to be ok," she stated as she hugged me.

Silent tears came across my face.

"People are talking about what transpired today. We will not tolerate this."

"Ms. Bush, I don't want him to lose his job because of this."

"Are you sure?"

"Yes, ma'am. Thank you for your concern. But, I just rather deal with him my way."

"Ok. Well, have a pleasant weekend."

"Thank you so much."

I left the room, appearing better. But that subsided as I was leaving. I got my phone out of my locker and left without saying bye to anyone else.

As I drove to New Orleans, I sensed I was calmer. I was experiencing more peace. Maybe because I was listening to music, the likes of Jill Scott, Anthony Hamilton, and Corinne Bailey Rae.

I pulled up at about 7. Walking up the steps; I stopped and talked to Uncle David and D3. Even though I seldom speak with them, I appreciated they loved me and respected me.

"So, how are the kids? Are they coming, Cuz?" I asked.

"Man, hell no," D3 expressed, "They are so chill. Both of their mamas are tripping too. But I can't sweat it. I'm still a playa."

"Yep," Uncle David stated, "You get your looks from me, son."

Shaking my head, I continued inside to talk to speak to Dani, Terrence, and Jackson.

"So who all is coming tomorrow?" I inquired.

"Well, Evette coming, ya know. I am excited for y'all to meet her. Ya know," Terrence blushed.

"Yeah, we know. Um, well, all of us that's here. And uh," Jackson cleared his throat, "Everybody on Uncle John's side. Including his favorite daughter- and son-in-law."

We didn't want to deal with them. Dani and I looked at each other; we took a deep breath. I looked at Momo Jean's picture and realized she would have wanted us to continue the traditions.

"Man, I am kinda ok with Regina and Jacob. But y'all, please keep Melissa's ass away from me." Terrence was emphatic about it.

"Lord, cousin, we gonna be nice."

"Yeah, speak for yourself."

There was no convincing him to be nice to Melissa. I had my reasons I didn't care for her. But his issue with her affected the entire family.

So I changed the subject. I asked, "What is everybody's role?"

Dani stated. "We are going to stores to shop for little decorations. She wants Saints colors, of course. My brother and daddy will grill. Big T will do the sides. Plus, Jackson will put the games together."

"Sounds like a plan," Jackson said. He smiled in agreement. Terrence agreed.

Just then, Uncle David and D3 came. "Anybody for UNO or pitty-pat?"

"Hey, I'm down. UNO first, though."

So we sat there playing UNO and pitty-pat hand for hand until Uncle David, D3, and Dani left.

My day started horribly. At Momo Jean's house, I was more at peace. My consciousness noticed time with my family mattered most.

THE NEXT MORNING I woke up to Dani calling me to inform me she was coming in 30 minutes. I had the house to myself. Terrence and Jackson were already out running their errands and getting food.

I washed up and put on a red and black Starter outfit and the comfy shoes from Rue 21. We were going to stores to shop. There was no reason to care about what I wear. I just wanted to be at ease.

"Knock, knock," Dani announced, tapping on the door. I opened it, "Boy, you are wearing Wally-"

"Dani, I am having a quality morning. This is not my party outfit. Relax. At least I…"

"Match," she said with her smart mouth, "But anyway, I came over here to talk to you about something before we leave."

"What's up?"

"I wanted to see how you are. I mean, since your co-worker did what he did? How are you?"

I took a long pause.

"Aiden Josiah?"

"Ok. I am not handling it well. The boy outed me to every-one. I wish I had not dropped a pill. It hurts because I suppose I'm a person with upstanding morals. I didn't…"

I started bawling. She hugged me.

"It's ok. I am here."

"I know, but now I gotta deal with Melissa and Jim and the rest of Uncle John's family. That's the primary reason Mama doesn't want to come around. That and her grief. I know Momo wants us to stay together. But, not like this."

"I feel you. I will be there. Promise you that."

She hugged me tighter. I also recognized that Terrence and Jackson had my back, too. I believed they would protect me.

WE LEFT and departed for Party City. We got all the black and gold decorations we could find. So next stop we made a run to was Dollar Tree. A lady was coming out of the store while we entered. Her head was down where you could see the details in her brown Ghana cornrow braids. Shades covered her eyes as she dropped a card.

"Miss, you dropped your…"

All I saw was light denim jeans, red heels, and the back of a crop top as she walked. She continued to strut to her Volkswagen Beetle convertible, which was metallic light blue. The jeans fit her. As she was getting in the car, she tilted her glasses down, winked, and smiled. It was Angèle. She looked different from the last time. When I picked the card up, she had left. I looked at it. It had the Roman numeral for XI and said secret societies. Through research, I googled it and learned it was the justice card in the New Orleans Voodoo Tarot. I put the card in my back pocket and walked inside the store.

Dani was in line. Right behind her were Jevaun and Indigo. I sighed. I did not want any drama.

"Hey, y'all."

He waved, and she rolled her eyes.

"Dani, you got everything?" I asked.

Dani stated, "Yeah. Oh, I invited them to the party too. But they declined because of work."

I bet that is, so I thought. The attendant rang her. He gave her the receipt with his number on it.

"I didn't ask for your number."

"Well, give it to him," He said. His teeth were so pearly white against his copper-toned skin.

"Oops!" Indigo squealed.

I heard Jevaun clear his throat like he disapproved, even though he was holding Indigo from behind.

"I'll think about it," I cheesed as I batted my eyelashes like the stepsisters off of Brandy's version of Cinderella.

"You doing the most." Dani carried on to give an explanation. "Sir, he will call you. Jay and Indi, it was pleasant to see y'all." She turned to me. "And, Loverboy, let's go. We gotta get back to the house."

Everyone in the store laughed at how Dani loud capped me. I just shook my head. We walked out with our items and got back to the car.

"Aiden Josiah. Tell me this. What the hell type of chemistry you and Jay got to where Indigo feels threatened?" She asked, "He definitely didn't like that young man flirting with you."

"Cousin, I'm not sure. I don't even talk to them anymore. It's weird. Let's just drop it and go have fun."

"Mm-hmm."

So It was 7:15. We got the house filled with black and gold balloons. Pandora was playing on the TV at a Neo-soul station with today's R&B. Uncle David and D3 had finished grilling. I was sitting and chilling in my black and gold patterned t-shirt and black Old Navy jeans.

"I am here!!!" Regina announced herself. "Happy birthday to me."

She stepped into the house in a bright gold light dress. 6-foot full-figured woman standing with an expresso skin tone was beautiful on the outside. But how she treats me makes her not as pleasant looking.

"Hi, Cousin. Happy birthday." I tried to put some excitement in my voice.

"Hmm. Remember, I am the queen. Not you. But thanks," she said with a remark full of shade, clutching her purse. She took out some disinfectant spray and sprayed in my direction. Then, in came her father, Uncle John. He came in the same height as her with his Saints t-shirt and black jeans. Of course, he didn't speak. I didn't care about talking to him either until I looked at Momo Jean's photo on the wall.

"Hey, Uncle John."

Nothing. When he sat on the couch, he said nothing.

I got up; The atmosphere was uncomfortable. So I proceeded to Terrence's room. They were in there, puffing and passing.

"Y'all uncle here," I said, pouting.

"Ah, little cuz. It's ok. Listen. Anybody get out of line, I got this," Terrence smirked. He reached under his bed and pulled out 9 mm.

"Put away that shit, man," Jack said. He kind of snapped. He didn't like guns.

"Yeah, Cuz. You, I fear those things." I was very squeamish around guns.

"Aww, man, y'all some scary, dog. But I feel you." He slid it back under the bed. "I guess we should go to entertain people."

We came out of the room; We advanced into the living room.

Uncle John gave daps to Jackson and Terrence, but pulled his hand back when he saw me. I just rolled my eyes.

"Everybody can come fix a plate now." Dani peaked her head into the living room.

Just then, Melissa, Jim, and Jacob came. I wished my mom were here. I sat in the corner and ate in the kitchen with Dani. The food was self-serve. When Jim got his food, he was still staring at me with lust. Melissa noticed and sucked her teeth at me. I peeked into the living room. It was nice that everybody was together for a joyous occasion. We all got our food and ate till our hearts' content.

"Aww, man. Aiden, what did we forget to buy?" Dani asked me.

"Alcohol!" everybody in the living room said with a shout.

"Well, it looks like I gotta go make a liquor run," Dani said before she gave an exclamation. "Big T!"

"Yeah!"

"2 words. Liquor Run."

"Damn, ok. I am coming."

She turned to me, "You are going to be ok?"

I nodded, yes. I knew Jackson was still here. So if anybody made me feel bad, he would be here.

"Hey, y'all, we bout to play a game of charades & guess who." Regina beckoned us to come into the living room.

Before the game started, Dani and Terrence left to go to the liquor store. Then Jackson got a call from one of his girl-friends. He made his way outside to see her. My perception switched to that I was alone.

"So," announced Regina. "This is how to play. Say or act out your clue. It can be anything you want. We guess the answer. Sounds fair?"

It seemed like a harmless game to play. I stood where the kitchen and living room met. So we were 5 minutes into the game. It was Regina's turn.

"So, I am wearing black and gold. I am about to die pretty soon." Regina's snicker gave off a dark clue who she was discussing.

Everybody looked around, confused. I was wondering why she even joked like that? So I waited for the next clue.

Regina set up her jokes to poke fun. "Y'all don't know. Ok. I am a supreme queen. But, this person is such a queen."

Everyone looked dead at me. Ugh, all of my support was outside. What was I going to say?

"Why would you say I am going to die soon?" I asked Regina.

"Because I got a call from my distant little cousin on my mom's side. Plus, Melissa found a pill in the bathroom earlier. You wanna share it, or shall I?" she mouthed off. She was waving this pill in the air.

It was the pill I used to take. I don't even take that drug anymore. Melissa must have gotten it from a particular place. That proved what I had known all along. Before I could give a rebuttal, she blurted it out.

"Momo Jean's baby got AIDS!"

My mouth gaped open in shock. "I don't have AIDS. I am HIV Positive."

My eyes wandered around for 2 seconds. I was looking at everyone's expressions. Jim's jaw dropped. Melissa looked stunned. Uncle David and D3 looked sad. Jacob had a sinister smile on his face.

I ran into Terrence's room and locked the door. I was in pain. She had embarrassed me in front of everyone. I didn't want to be here. This life was one I didn't want to live. I had focused on my pain and remembered what Terrence said. I went under his bed and pulled out his beretta. No was a word that sounded loud in my head. I didn't listen to it. Ding! Ding!

I got a notification from Shamar. The fuck was he messaging me for now. I had been messaging him and giving him his space. Of all times he chooses to message me, it is now. He did not message me before, so fuck him. I hid the gun and walked out of the room. The first people I meet were Uncle David and D3. They were standing outside the door, waiting for me.

"Nephew, you ok?" Uncle David had a concerned look on his face after what he overheard.

"Man, look, you are ok, huh?" D3 asked.

"Look, I love y'all, but I gotta go."

I wanted to get away from everybody. My head and heart need clearing. I didn't want to deal with the pain anymore. I ignored everybody else and made a B-Line straight to Regina.

"So Glenn called you to tell you that? I never realized y'all associated with each other. Plus," I paused, "Plus was family. You don't even like gay people, so why would you listen to him?"

She said with a heinous roar, "I still don't like the gays. But, he is on my mother's side. Y'all didn't make us feel like family after what happened so."

"I was freaking two years old. But ok. You never have to deal with me anymore. That pill you have. I haven't taken those in years."

I moved past her to the door. Before I went to my car, I saw Jackson sitting in a 2013 Nissan Altima that was blue.

I knocked on the window, and he let the window down.

"Cuz, I'm bout to go home. I'll text you when I make it." I gave my cousin a reason. He would ask me what was wrong if I sounded too nervous.

"The people?"

"The people. So I gotta go. Love you."

"I love you too, Cuz."

I WALKED AWAY from the car before I started weeping. Nobody was on the porch to ask me what was the matter. It was like I'm in the clear. I got in my car.

Ding! Ding!

It was messages from Shamar.

You answer me. What's up?

Aiden, this is not like you. Answer me. I am here.

I cut my phone off. My mind was cognizant that location services were on the phone. There was no way I would let them track my whereabouts. I didn't want to hear from Terrence, let alone Joanne or Dani. My car sped off into the night; I sensed I was going to take my pain away.

10

ON THE LAKEFRONT

I was riding in silence. The hateful thoughts of my cousin Regina played over and over in my head. Shamar's rejection of what I wanted stirring in my mind. Glenn's revelation and my mistreatment at work replayed time and time again. I drove to the lakefront. That is where I would find peace. I was going to hell if I was gay. That was the lesson taught to me growing up. If I took my life, I was going to hell. So my thoughts were I was going to hell, anyway. So let me speed up the process.

I parked in what I thought was a secluded spot. Second thoughts flooded my head as I glanced at the gun. I looked in my rear-view mirror for half a second. I gasp, then I blinked. And he was not there. I rubbed my eyes. I picked up the gun and put it in my lap. My feelings were I wanted the pain to go away. I thought this indeed was the end.

I looked over, and I shook my head. This was the second time. I saw someone who looked like Shamar. He stared at me for a second with an angry face; then, he disappeared. I put the gun back on the passenger seat.

I was getting freaked out. Maybe I just wanted Shamar to come and save me. Perhaps I wanted to remember our memories and talks. I sensed my mind was playing tricks on me.

I picked up the gun again and sat it in my lap. Then my radio popped on. The song was Whitney Houston's "You Were Loved" off of The Preacher's Wife soundtrack. I listened for a while. I cried because I felt I was wrong. But I could not ignore my pain. I cut the song off.

My phone jumps on with the same song. There was nervousness in my fingers at this point. It was getting harder and harder to end it all. I cut the phone off, throwing it on the seat.

BAM! Bam! Bam!

Man, why can't I be alone? I rolled down the window and started crying.

"So you gonna unlock the car and let me in?" he said.

"Yeah," I sniffled.

I unlocked the car and sat in the seat. He looked at me with disappointment in his hazel eyes. He had a towel.

"Let me take that," Jevaun stated. He removed the gun from my lap. He put it under the seat after wrapping it in a towel.

We started talking at the same time. Chuckling, we agreed I should go first.

"So, how did you find me?" I asked him.

"You gotta promise me you won't think I am crazy. That you will not blow up on me," he stated.

"Ok."

"Shamar told me."

The laugh that came was so obnoxious. I was in disbelief.

"Damn, Wah deh suh funny?" He asked. I knew he was getting mad when he started talking Jamaican Patois.

"Ok," I paused, "So how did he tell you? Uh, better question. How do you know Shamar?"

"He woke me up out of my sleep. Shamar is my dead brother."

I gave him a funny, puzzled look. This man did not tell that story. Shamar was his brother. Not only that, but Shamar is his dead brother. I was getting furious.

Jevaun pulled out his phone and showed me pictures of him and Shamar together. I finally looked at Jevaun, realizing they resemble each other. He described his family tree, beginning with his mom being Jamaican. Shamar's dad was African American. But His dad was Creole, Italian, and African American.

Then he got to the painful part. He explained to me someone killed Shamar last year. The police reasoned it was a suicide. He still believed his brother would not do that. He further explained that the lakefront was his brother's favorite place, that the last thing Shamar wore was an all-black Adidas suit.

I had always wondered why I only saw him twice. Both times he wore the same thing. It shocked and puzzled me. I calmed down.

"There is something I need to do first before we continue," He stated emphatically.

He dialed a number, they answered, and he handed me the phone.

"Never do that shit again. And bring Terrence's gun back," Dani screamed at me over the phone.

"I'm sorry," I said, with tears coming through my eyes.

"It's going to be ok. Everyone knows now about your status. We, the ones that love you, will help you. Plus, I am going to tell you what happened while you weren't here. I'm going to call Tee Joanne and tell her you're ok."

"Ok. Thank you."

I give him his phone. It annoyed me he called Dani, but I was also grateful. I realized killing myself would solve nothing. In fact, it would have caused more family dissension.

"So, back to you and my brother. How did you even meet?" Jay asked me.

So I TOLD him how I met the ghost of his brother. Stories of me meeting him rambled off my tongue. I realized the truth is what I needed to tell.

"So that night when you got drunk and called me Shamar. You freaked me out."

"That night, I promise I saw him."

"Dang. We are missing something here. There has to be a link here. He was one always with a plan."

"Yeah. Your girlfriend told me you had a brother that died. She never said Shamar's name. Wait, does Indigo know you are here?"

"Nope. We broke up."

"I hope I had nothing to do with it."

He chuckled. He explained she was his best friend. She knew he was bi or was at least attracted to guys. He was never interested in guys until he met me at the concert.

She had been threatening to tell his mother, who is very homophobic. His mother always suspected that he was, but not his older brother. Shamar was her tough boy, and he was the soft one she wanted to toughen up.

"Look, I like you a lot. But I'm positive. You're younger and I..." I was giving an explanation.

He put his fingers on my lips to silence me. "Listen, I am ok with that. We will figure everything out. Don't worry; we'll cross that bridge together. But I am not going anywhere."

"Ok," I said with a sigh. "You want to shake hands on that?"

"Nah, I rather we create our own." He gave this raised eyebrow and winked.

We created our signature handshake: 2 fist bumps consecutively, locked pinkies, fist to chest, and deuces/peace sign. Does this mean I have a boyfriend? Is this even right? I just know it felt great to have someone reciprocate these feelings.

"So we going to park your car and leave it in the morning. Come spend the night. No funny stuff." He had to make a joke.

I NODDED and texted Dani where I was going to be. So we parked my car in a spot. It looked like I was a student on the UNO campus. He got Terrence's gun and put it in his car since I hopped in his 2017 black Dodge Charger. I smiled and grinned at him the whole time. He turned on the radio before we could start riding. I felt sick.

"Man, can you please turn the station?" I said.

"What's wrong with that song?" he asked me as he was bobbing his head.

I turn the song off real quick. He looked at me like he was a tad mad.

"Wah di fuck yuh duh dat for?" Jay responded, a little peeved.

"I do not support or listen to that artist."

I went into detail about how Glenn hurt me and sent me a video of that artist saying what she said. On Instagram Live, the artist got so mad at someone that she wished AIDS on the person's mother. I understood where the artist's anger stemmed. It did not give her cause to wish a condition or virus on someone. Whether she knows it, she had fans who listened and bought her music who go through that. For her to wish that on someone disgusted me as a human being. It was uncalled for her to make that statement. So, I, as a consumer, stopped buying her music. I know I am only one person, but I stand for what I believe. People stopped listening to R. Kelly because of what he allegedly did. I compared it to that. I should be able to boycott that artist for what she said.

"So what you do when they play her music in the club?" He was so curious about it.

"Well, I either stand there and roll my eyes or sit down somewhere. I mean, I don't wish her any harm or less success—many blessings to her. I don't care if you or anyone else listens to her. But, I am not playing or enjoying her music until she apologizes for that comment."

"MAN, let me plug my phone and put on my duets playlist."

"Quit playing. I have one. Let's see if we have similar taste."

We pull off to go to his house; "Like You" by Ciara and Bow Wow was booming through his speakers. Between our lists, we had many of the same songs. It was crazy. From Roberta Flack and Peabo Bryson to Janet and Busta, we went through the lists back and forth. Of course, he sang the male parts, and I sang the female roles. We both kinda got emotional listening to "Take Care" by Drake and Rihanna as we pulled up to his house.

"Come on," Jay beckoned.

"Dark Side of the Moon" came on. So I begged him to listen to it and sing it with me, and he did. The emotions and lyrics that Nicki and Wayne conveyed in the song were touching and special to me.

We got out of the car and I followed him inside. It was a friendly house. It had the same general layout as Momo Jean's house. Along the walls, I saw pictures of the three of them. I saw more pictures of Shamar and their mom without him. He had hung his head when I noticed that.

I walked to this door. Something was drawing me closer to it. "So whose room is this?"

"Don't go in there. That's Shamar's room. My mada would get real mad. She goes into his room to feel close to him," Jay empathetically said.

"You trust me?"

"Yes."

~

I OPEN the door to Shamar's room. I sat on the bed. Jay experienced shock, but he sits beside me. In Shamar's room, it's nothing but sports articles and pictures of him and Jevaun.

"Did Shamar know about you?"

"Yeah, I talk to him about everything. He knew about me, and I knew about him. When my mother would whoop me, he would step in. I miss him. He truly was my best friend."

He was talking about Shamar when I perceived something under my feet. I reached under the bed and pulled it out. It was a journal by Shamar.

"I really don't want you going through my brother's stuff," Jay cautiously stated.

The journal was in my lap until it slid on the floor, face-up, and started flipping pages. Jay looked spooked. I picked it up and started reading it. Shamar had detailed how he had seen his teacher for a couple of months. He took detailed notes on when they would meet up. Then I skimmed the reason given for their breakup. I had to read it out loud because I observed my pain.

"Jay, it says here your brother was going to Weld NOLA Tech," I said. I read. "So I wanted to be with my professor—one problem: his marital status. He didn't want me to, but I was going to tell his wife. I love JD, and he is what I want."

"What's wrong?" Jay asked. It concerned him because the pages were getting wet with my tears.

"Jevaun. Listen," I tried to wipe my tears and catch my breath, "Us meeting is no accident. I need you to hear me out. A deacon raped me at my church when I was 18. I never reported it." I paused. "So years later, I find out that my cousin married the deacon who raped me. So now your brother has an affair with my cousin's husband, who is also my rapist. Jay, JD is Jim Daniels. Jim Daniels is my rapist. Jim Daniels is the reason I am HIV Positive. He is the person who I am sure is 100% responsible for Shamar's death."

"Enuh weh he is?" Jay said in a fury. "Weh a di motherfucker? Mia gwine kill him wid fi mi bare han dem."

He broke, crying to the floor. I got on the floor after him. We held each other. We let all the hurt and pain go, releasing it with our tears.

"The notebook is not enough evidence to get him charged. But I have an idea."

"Listen, let's go to my room. You sleep in my bed, and I will sleep on the floor, and I will tell my mother everything."

I said goodbye to Shamar and thanked him for bringing me another friend.

"Here." Jay gave me everything I need to shower and sleep. "The bathroom is here. The soap that I use is there."

"Thanks."

"No problem."

While I was in the shower, my mind raced. Thoughts of the day circled my head. I progressed from running from my fears to facing them. I was learning to stand up for myself.

My feet tiptoed to his room, dressed in his T-shirt and pajamas.

"U sure this is ok?" I asked. I was nervous about spending the night.

"Yeah." He looked at me and kissed me on my forehead. I cheesed. "Goodnight."

So WHILE HE was taking his shower, I drifted to sleep. Shamar came into my dreams. It was like we were sitting in his car at the lakefront—just me and him.

"Fi mi bredda is pretty awesome, huh?" Shamar said.

"Why didn't you tell me he was your brother? And your shirt is white." I had noticed he wasn't wearing the black shirt anymore. I was dumbfounded and confused.

"The truth will come to light now. It will set me free." He gave as a reason. "Including yours and my brother's. I need one more favor. Retrieve my phone. It's on the lakefront, and I will lead you to it. Whenever time permits."

"Does it matter the day?"

"No, it does not. Mi need yuh tuh cova yuh ed wid yuh arms. Wake Up!"

"What?"

"Cova yuh ed. Wake Up! Wake Up!"

I opened my ears. It was earlier morning…

11

THE AFTERMATH & THE 2 MOMS

"Cova yuh ed. Wake Up! Wake Up!"

I opened my ears. It was early morning.

Shamar's voice faded out, turning to a powerful woman's voice.

"Wake Up! Wake Up!" she said. Then she hit my arm with a cast-iron skillet as I covered my head.

"Ow!!!"

Jay woke up, jumped up, and grabbed his mother.

His voice echoed loudly. "Go into the bathroom. Lock the door."

∾

I DID what I was told. My feet could not go any faster. I tried to run as fast as I could down the hall. As soon as I locked the door, I turned around. I looked in the mirror, and a figure became clear. It was Shamar.

"Stay here. You will know when it's safe to come out. This ain't the first time I protected you in a bathroom."

I nodded my head in agreement. He disappeared. Then I pondered on what he said. I realized he was the one who scared Jim at the church. I chuckled at the fact that he saw a ghost. Outside the bathroom door, I overheard their conversation.

"Leggo ah mi. Jevaun, Yuh really get ah chichi man bwoy eena fi mi house?" She angrily questioned him after he let her go. "A yuh losing yuh fucking mind?"

She stood there, looking at her son. Her skin was dark ebony. Her 5'1" frame was small in stature. The attitude she had was setup like she was 10 feet.

"Madda Dat a nuh nice. He a helping mi. Wi really," he responded. He exited his room, going to the living room.

"How a di chichi man bwoy supposed tuh help me?" she shrugged, following him. "Maybe he a helping yuh gwaana hell. Damn Sodomite."

"Madda Dat a enuff. He figured out ahuu kill Shamar," Jay had to shout for her to understand.

"Duh nuh mention fi mi son eena regards tuh dat batty bwoy. let mi si wah he seh." It intrigued her to find out what knowledge I had.

"Mada sidung yah. Mi gwine git him suh yuh can hear him out," Jay stated.

He knocked on the bathroom door. "It's me."

I let him in. He hugged me.

"Listen, ok. I'm taking baby steps. I need you to keep the journal in your possession at all times. You trust me?" he asked me.

I nodded my head. He opened the door, and I swiftly located the journal. I followed him out to the kitchen. I was still wearing his clothes I slept in.

"Hello," I said, extending my right hand as I walked closer to her.

"Nuh touch mi."

I heard Shamar say in a whisper to me, "Go outside. Sit on the steps. I will help my brother get through to her."

"It was a pleasure meeting you. I am going to sit outside," I stated.

"Dat chichi man bwoy nuh kno nutten bout fi mi son," she sang as I walked out the door and sat on the steps. "Now yuh. Wah mek yuh an Indigo tap talking? Yuh betta nuh utter dem words dat will sen yuh tuh hell."

"Indigo kno mi did ah bisexual suh did fi mi bredda," Jay huffed, "He kno jus lakka yuh kno bout mi. He kno yuh wud'n akcep mi. Buh yuh didn't kno bout him. He…"

She slapped him mid-sentence. "Fi mi son did nah batty man. Yuh will nah disrespect unnu dead bredda. Yuh hear me? eff yuh waah tuh bi batty man den yuh git di fuck outta fi mi house."

"Suh bi ih. Mi will still help yuh out wid di bills." Jevaun said in a cry as he withdrew to his room to pack. There was no use in wasting his breath on his mother anymore. He packed up most of his belongings except for some clothing. The last thing he took was his favorite photo. He wiped the little dust off his picture with Shamar. She would never understand how he or Shamar felt. He would miss his mom, but he would rather find his own way.

"Bwoy guh put yuh clothes bac inna di room. Weh yuh tink unnu a go?," Alvita asked.

"Mi luv yuh buh mia deh leff." He had shed tears.

Alvita escalated, "Fi mi son ah batty man boy! Fuck yuh. Yuh a nah fi mi son. Mi cyaan believe yuh cum out fi mi pussy."

Jevaun could see his mother with tears silently coming down. She bullied him and called him all kinds of names.

Once he was outside, she scolded him with those same names. He just kept moving.

"Help me put my bags up, please?" Jay asked me.

I gave him a puzzled gaze. Did I cause him to get kicked out? Had this been brewing? So many thoughts ran through my head, but I calmed down. Her attacking words had now turned to him and me. I just got in the car.

"You ready?" Jay was nervous.

"Yep, you're going to be ok."

When Alvita retreated inside, she was still cursing and angry. A wall picture of the 3 of them that was in a frame fell. The glass from it shattered all over the floor. Another image fell; however, this one was completely intact. It was just of the two brothers. She thought it was just a mere coincidence and carried on to clean her mess.

APPARENTLY, Momo Jean's house was just a few blocks from Jevaun's mom's house. When we arrived, Dani and Jackson were on the porch. Walking up to them, they stopped their conversation.

"Hey, y'all. So where is Big T?" I asked.

"So you not going to address what happened, Aiden Josiah? You better be glad we went to church today. We are not sweeping it under the rug." Dani gave it to me straight. I hung my head in regret. "Hi, Jevaun. This is our cousin, Jackson."

They spoke to each other and gave each other dap. We proceeded inside the house where Terrence and I assume the girl sitting with him was Evette. Terrence gave me the biggest hug while he shed tears, and we introduced each other's person to one another. Evette was a full-figured girl with cocoa skin and brown hair. Had I not been out of it at Momo Jean's funeral, I would have definitely recognized her.

"So my nigga where is my gun?" Terrence said in his stern voice. He couldn't believe I was daring enough to take his tool. "Say Bruh. Never do that shit again."

"I am aware. I won't, I promise. The gun is in the car."

"Ok cool."

"Y'all tell me what happened after I left."

An awkward silence came through, sweeping their mouths. It was odd.

"All of you. Please do not go all at once." I said as a sarcastic joke.

"Man, that shit was not funny what you pulled. You should thank Evette, ya know. I might have been in jail." Terrence responded.

"Aht Aht, allow me to tell it," Dani said.

Dani precedes to tell the story of what happened after I left.

~

So, Dani and Terrence had come back 20 minutes after I left. They had brought the liquor back and also picked up Evette so she could meet the family. So when they walked in, everybody was acting strange.

"So, how was the game? Why y'all not playing?" Dani asked her family.

Her father spoke. "It's because the lovely birthday girl here revealed that Aiden had HIV to the family."

Terrence looked shocked, and Evette shed tears. He wasn't aware of why she was crying, so he just held her. Dani was irate.

She got straight in Regina's face. Dani said for a comment, "Is that why you were spraying Lysol? That is uninformed and insensitive."

Regina just shrugged her nonchalant shoulders.

Dani wanted to smack her, but her thoughts turned into worry.

Evette was still in tears, and Terrence had walked to his bedroom. He looked under his bed and noticed his gun was missing. He came stomping out the room.

"So who has my gun?"

Everybody looked at him crazily until he repeated himself.

"So who has my gun?"

Melissa snarled to Terrence, "hmm, I guess your favorite cousin took it."

Jim shook his head. "Wife, that was not nice. I hope he does nothing to himself."

Dani rolled her eyes. "Yeah, listen to your husband on this one." The sadness came into her voice. "Terrence, I think Aiden has your gun."

He goes straight to Regina. "If my cousin does something to himself, On PawPaw and my dad, I'm gonna fuck you up."

"Don't talk to my daughter like that defending that faggot. Shit, he going to hell anyway," Uncle John said with a low bark.

"Old man, listen. You, my uncle and all, but I ain't got to respect you. That is still your sister's son."

"I do not care about him being Joanne's son. That little…"

Dani said with a shout, "Oh my God, Aunt Joanne. Y'all stop fighting now. I gotta try to call him. I can't deal with it, and calling her is not an option."

She came outside to call to me. Just as my voicemail came on, Jackson was coming up the stairs.

"Jack, did you see Aiden when he left?"

"Yeah, He told me he was going home. He couldn't deal with something related to the folks, and he bounced. Why? What's wrong?"

She sobs. "Regina revealed to the entire family that he had HIV. So apparently, he let himself in Terrence's room and grabbed his gun and left."

Jackson looked at her strangely. "So you're saying my cousin has that shit?"

She gave him a dirty stare. "Look, your cousin has HIV and not that shit. So what?! He is still Aiden. You cannot get it from him. I will help educate you on everything that I know."

"Hm, how long have you known?"

"Since the concert."

"Man, that's that…"

"That what? How could he come to Terrence or you? Then the fact is this. It would have been a bigger burden on him. Y'all would find the person. Then newscasters would inform us of their demise. You understand that. Plus, how he got it is his story to tell," Dani gave him her reasoning.

"I feel bad. I wish I wasn't talking to that girl…"

"He is going to be ok."

They moved back inside to join the rest of the family.

"I was really enjoying the game," Melissa whined, "I was enjoying family time."

"Bitch, my cousin might kill himself over what your sister revealed, and you worried bout some game? Everybody get out," Terrence yelled.

"Now you want to call my other daughter a bitch. Young Blood…"

"Man, look, Uncle John, you gotta go. And Jacob, you better stay seated." Terrence's tone was harsh to his uncle before warning his cousin.

Everyone left except for Terrence, Jackson, Dani, and Evette. They prayed for me. At that moment, Dani got the phone call from Jevaun.

"So cousin, that's what happened when you left," Dani finished.

I was so overwhelmed. It didn't surprise me what Uncle John said.

"Part of the story is missing. So Evette," I said with a grin, turning my attention to her, "Why did you cry?"

"Well, I had a gay uncle who was like a big brother to me. We called him Plum because he said Peaches was too flamboyant for him."

We all laughed.

"So, Uncle Plum, as much as I loved him." She had to pause. "He did heroin. He hooked up with guys. It wasn't consistent. He would get tested every three months. So during nine months, there were no guys he was pursuing. He was still sharing needles to get high."

"So that's how he got it?" Jevaun asked.

"Yes." Tears filled her eyes. "He called me when he found out. I told him I loved him. He told me he loved me, and he was going to Baton Rouge to be away from judgmental family. He jumped off the Mississippi Bridge that day."

Terrence held her as she put her head on his shoulder.

"It was important for me to meet you so I could tell you your life is worth it."

"Thank you, Evette, for sharing. I am stronger now that I have my homie here," I nudged Jevaun, "and my family. Thank you all so much for loving me."

"So I think we should celebrate the family. Do over this Sunday?" Dani asked hesitantly. "With all the family? Brunch at 2?"

"All the family?" Jackson asked unsurely.

"Yep. All of them."

I hopped up. I stated, "I'm down, and my mama will be present."

"Cool. And Jay. You better be here," Dani said as she smirked and side-eyed.

"I will be." He said for a reply. I smiled.

Jackson moved outside, so I came out after him.

We sat on the steps together.

"Bruh, why did you lie? I would have blamed the people. I would have blamed myself. If you would have…"

"Jack. You and Big T are more like brothers to me. I'm already gay. Y'all treat me no different. But telling you both that I was positive too. I didn't want to feel rejected."

"You, my little brother. I got to have somebody to help me pick on Terrence. So do you know who…"

"The truth is Momo Jean and your Tee Joanne had knowledge of it. I told Dani and now Jevaun. What happened, and with who? I can't tell you that now. Just trust me."

"Should I after the stunt you pulled?"

"Well, Ok. You got me there."

"Nah, I feel you Cuz. You know me. I'll try to find whoever it was. Oh, Jevaun, he cool people. If y'all go that route, I ain't wearing no dress to comply."

"Bro, what the hell!" I busted out in laughter.

Everybody came out.

"Say, Jay, can you unlock your car so I can get my gun?" Terrence asked.

Jevaun hit the button, and he walked down the steps to retrieve it.

"So we on for Sunday?" I asked.

Everybody answered with a resounding yes.

So Jay and I said our goodbyes, and we set out to get my car.

"You think she will let me stay?" He wanted to have that information.

"I think so. Believe me."

WE ARRIVED AT MY CAR. He followed me back from New Orleans to Marais Vert. He was about to meet my favorite person: my mommy, Joanne.

Joanne was standing out on the porch when we pulled up to the house. I guess Dani had texted her to let her know I was on the way home.

"Hi, mama," I said, walking up to her.

She grabbed me. She held me in the tightest hug ever.

"You better never think that again." My mother said in a mumble. "If you do, I will do it myself. I brought you into this world. It's my right to take you out of it."

I gulped. I was conscious that my mother had unconditional love for me. It was apparent I did not realize how much.

"You are ok, and I am too," she said in a soft tone. She let me breathe more.

She let me go. I turned and motioned Jevaun to come.

"Whoa. Aht Aht! Who is this fellow you bringing for me?" She asked. She knew how to joke with me.

"For you?"

"Yes, for me," she said. She turned to him. "Would you like something to eat?"

"Your mom is funny. Yes, ma'am."

"Come on in. I love your accent. Plus, I know my child. You two have an interesting story."

I looked at him, and he looked at me. Laughter and amusement were all that escaped from our eyes and mouth.

So I caught up with mom. I spoke to her about how I met Jevaun and how he was there for me. He was proper when introducing himself and told her about his life plans. What I didn't expect was for him to open up, especially about his mother. A sorrowful look came across her face.

"So what are plans with you and my son being friends?" She asked.

I covered my eyes because I didn't want either of them to see my face.

"Well, your son is my best friend. He understands me. I appreciate him and care about him a lot." He had no doubt when he said it.

"Well, you seem like a bright young man. Now, I believe in this word of God. I have done my best by raising my son. There are some things I will not quote-unquote accept. But I'm not judging because I'm not in you guys' shoes. I would much rather see my son have a relationship with God and deal with his sins than him committing suicide and me having to bury my baby," Joanne asserted with tears running.

Me and Jevaun both teared up.

"So," she exhaled a sigh of relief, "Rule 1. You are moving into Aiden's room."

"Huh? Where am I sleeping?" I wondered out loud.

"Boy, I am not finished. Shut. Up." My mom had a small twinkle on her face. "Now, where was I?"

"The part you said I could stay," Jevaun smirked.

She remembered, "Ah, yes. Aiden, your moving into Momo Jean's room. Rule 2. In front of me, Y'all can act like brothers, but cha can't act like lovers."

"What?!" I said so hard. "So you tryna rap like Nicki?"

"No fool. Like MC Lyte."

Jevaun snickered then got quiet, "Your mom is funny. I kinda wish she was my mom."

"My 3rd rule is for you, Jevaun, is for you to call me Majo, short for Mama Joanne. It will always stand unless you disrespect me and I put you out. I guess you are my son now," she said with grace.

Jevaun got up from his seat and hugged her.

I was smiling from ear to ear.

"Now, besides rule number 2. Suppose I smell or feel any of that hanky panky stuff going happening. I'm putting BOTH y'all asses out. These walls can talk. So respect the house, please."

The laughter befell the room.

Jevaun went to get all his stuff. Mama and I progressed to move clothes out of my room. We needed to put them in Momo Jean's room.

"That young man needs love. He has a noble head on his shoulders," she said to me.

"Thanks, mom, for being there for him and me," I said. My smile beamed from ear to ear. "There is something you need to know. We think Jim killed his brother."

My mother stopped dead in her tracks. "What?!"

"Yes. I am going to confront him on Sunday. I know you haven't been back..."

"Say no more. Everybody going to be there?"

"Yes. Ok."

She breathed heavily and nodded.

"I guess I have to face my fears too," she said with a sigh.

We finished moving all my clothes. Jevaun came in, and we did a family hug before helping him moved into his temporary room. It thrilled me. I still sensed what was to come.

12

OFF MY CHEST

I woke up early Sunday morning just thinking about how life could be. I looked at the nightstand and smiled. There was a picture of Momo Jean and me sitting there in landscape position.

"Well, Momo, I will stand up to him." I got on my knees and prayed. "Dear Lord, please give me the strength to stand up to those who hurt me. Help me heal this hurt. Please also, if you can, guide my tongue. Amen."

Getting up from the floor, I tiptoed to the bathroom.

This week had its challenges for Jevaun. He had been traveling back and forth with no complaints. Jay would see Indigo at work, but she wouldn't speak to him. He would come home solemn. I wished things could have been better between them.

However, the issues with his mother were even more heart-breaking. Jay told me about how he tried to visit her. He traveled to his mom's, leaving some money. He knocked on her door and stayed there for an hour. Soon as Alvita heard him start his engine, she peeped outside and took the money out of her mailbox. She never even so much as waved at her son. I felt terrible about how things went with his mother.

But I was fortunate to share Joanne with him. Hell, he kind of pushed me out of my spot. They always ganged up on me. I finished cleaning myself up and snuck to my old room. He was still sleeping with a smile on his face. I decided not to wake him just yet. My feet pranced lightly to my mother's room, and I cracked her door. She was sound asleep as well. So I went back to my room and got my clothes ready for church.

My RINGTONE FOR DANI SOUNDED. She usually isn't up at 6 in the morning. I guess she was getting ready for brunch.

Cousin. I was up and couldn't sleep. I want to let you know I am so proud of you. Regina and Uncle John are still here because of Hurricane Olga. Jim and Melissa say they were coming. I convinced Jacob to come by. I'm just praying that everything doesn't go left. See you again soon; I'm very proud of you.

I messaged back.

Aw Cousin. Thank you. Love you so much. Thank you for always being in my corner. I couldn't do it without you.

I waited for them to get up because we were attending the 8 AM Sunday service. I was nervous about attending the service. My anxiety was getting the better of me, so I just continually pressed my suit.

My mother knocked and entered my room because I cracked the door.

"Now, mommy!" I said out loud. I softened my tone not to wake Jevaun down the hall. "How you knock and open the door?"

"Because it is my house," she said, walking into my room. It always amazed me how she acted as though I didn't get my smart mouth from her. I just shook my head. "I see that you're making sure you look great for church. But are you sure you can handle the brunch?"

"Oh, mother. You really don't want to deal with your brother?"

"It's not so much of that. I don't want to catch sight of Jim. The prison doesn't need an exquisite woman held behind its bars. You know, such as myself."

"I think we will be fine," I said with a hearty laugh.

Just then, I looked up, hearing a knock at my open door. It was Jay, holding his suit on his arm. "Good Morning, Majo. Good Morning A.J. A.J., you think that you could iron my clothes, please?"

"Yeah, I got you."

"Thanks." He flashed them teeth, and my heart melted.

"Mmhmm. I figured you were the soft one. So domestic." My mother was chuckling and leaving out my room as I gasped for air, laughing at her.

We all cleaned ourselves up and left for church. Once there, we walked in with stares and fingers pointed at us. One member asked my mother who Jevaun was. She gave that church member a face that made them realize they shouldn't ask any more questions.

We sat down in the pews, looking like a family. Joanne was wearing a Modern Elegance dress in navy blue. Jay fit his Royal Indigo Cobalt suit nicely. I finished our family look by donning a blue Twisted Tailor suit. As usual, we carried on through the service; we weren't aware of who the speaker was today. The associate minister announced Pastor McKee would be the next voice we hear after the soloist. The voice heard was a familiar one. Bianca McKee sang "Deliver Me" with such conviction and richness.

Pastor McKee then walked up to the podium and began his sermon. He named it "Forgiveness is Better than Sacrifice". He pulled out a plethora of scriptures where God requires us to forgive those who hurt us. Being the bigger person was a central message. He made it clear with we do not forgive, then God will not forgive us. This point makes us sacrifice or put in jeopardy our spots in heaven. I thought the message was perfect. Reiterating what will happen was correct.

When service let out, Jay tapped me on the shoulder. "You listened to the sermon?"

"Yes." I nodded my head. "I feel like releasing it is the right thing."

"Come on, boys," my mother chimed in, "I believe all have some forgiveness to spread in the city."

All I could do was smile. It was time.

Even though she heard that sermon, my mother tried her best not to travel to the city. Jay and I convinced her to drive her car. I knew we would stay longer, but we would let her lead us down. She side-eyed us and agreed. We freshened up and drove down to the city. Before leaving, I sent a quick text to Dani that her Tee Joanne would make us late, but we were on our way.

WE PULLED up to Momo Jean's house at 2:30. My mom walked in; then, we followed suit. Jim saw her first and slithered his way to the restroom. Everybody was eating.

"Hello, everyone. Some of you have not met my other son. Family, this is Jevaun," my mother said. She had made me proud of introducing him in that way.

"Man, she on some..." Uncle John said with a mutter under his breath. Regina rolled her eyes.

"Look, brother. I went to church today. We will get along today." Joanne batted her eyes hard at him and then turned to Uncle David, who embraced her with a warm hug.

"Say, son. What's wrong?" Uncle John asked his seed.

Jacob was fidgety. I never saw him act that way. He could not stay still.

"Hey, don't I recognize you?" Jay asked him, "You were in school with my brother. You ok?"

"Oh yeah," Jacob said. He was still squirming a lot. "I'm cool. Your brother was, um..."

I knew he was fake pondering. The shaking of his leg was getting to me.

"Shamar. It was Shamar." Jevaun stated.

"Yeah, he was a cool person, man. I'm sorry for your loss." Jacob then gave a funny glare to Jim, who was coming out of the bathroom. I was so puzzled by his actions.

Jay and I walked into the kitchen where Dani, Terrence, Evette, and Jackson were. The spread of eggs, fresh fruit, vegetables, sausage, and sandwiches looked splendid. We ate in there. It was about 4 PM, and everyone was getting along. I wish I didn't have to break this family togetherness.

"Dani, I'm ready," I stated. She looked at me and nodded.

In the living room, Jacob gritted his teeth. He snuck out of the house before everybody started entering the living room. He texted Jim.

Say, how did he meet Shamar's brother?

Jim wrote back. *I have no idea, Little Nut. Calm down.*

As he entered his vehicle, he shook his head. He realized something big was going to happen.

EVERYBODY CROWDED in the living room except for Jacob.

"I want to thank everybody for coming. It's great to be with y'all. Really it is."

Everyone was listening to me, but Uncle John's family. They were carrying on side conversations, ignoring me. My mother was sitting close to Uncle John, and open-handed slapped him upside his head. He just looked at her. Terrence glanced at him like, don't think about hitting his aunt.

"Now that I have everyone's attention. Thanks to everyone who fixed brunch. I wanted to see all of you. The last family gathering caused me much pain. I was going to end my life. But somebody reminded me I had a life worth living."

"This brat is getting on my nerves," Regina said in a mumble. Melissa nodded and laughed.

I got so furious. The tears started flowing because I experienced being disrespected. "This brat would not have tried to commit suicide had you not outed me being positive. And Melissa, you sit there with sunshades covering your black eyes. You cannot laugh. At all. Because how would you feel if your cousin married your rapist?! By the way, he is also a murderer!"

I started weeping. The room grew still. Then chaos ensued. Jackson and Jay lunged towards Jim. They started fighting. Uncle David and D3 broke up the brawl. Regina couldn't believe what she overheard. Melissa stood there in shock. She finally put 2 and 2 together and looked at her husband in disgust.

"EVERYBODY SHUT UP AND LISTEN." Terrence was crying. He stomped back into the living room. Evette was pleading with him. Everybody stood still because Terrence had his gun pointed at Jim and Melissa.

"I have always hated you," Terrence said with disgust. "You were always mad at Aiden because he took your spot as the spoiled one. Do you remember what you did? Huh? You took my father and PawPaw away from the family?"

"Terrence, how would-"

"Shut the fuck up. I always relive that dreadful day. It was your 5th-grade graduation, and you forgot to pick up your cap. My father and PawPaw didn't want you embarrassed. They left to get your cap. On the way back, they get hit by someone who ran a red light. I lost my father and PawPaw! Now, you married somebody who raped my little cousin."

"Terrence!" My mother stepped to the side of him. "Don't pull no trigger. Listen to me. Evette is standing beside you. You have done a superb job of protecting my son. I know you feel she is responsible for PawPaw and Connor. But, it was an unfortunate accident that impacted all of us. Don't throw your life away. Things are going well for you now. This is not the way."

He lowered his gun. Uncle John was in disbelief. Regina just hung her head, showing a lot of remorse.

When I looked at Jim, he had a swollen eye and busted lip.

"Well, this was an eventful evening. I killed no one. Aiden, stop playing the victim, and I am not positive," he said in front of everybody.

"So you're not going to deny raping me? That's cute. But God bless you. I hope my cousin leaves you and takes everything you got. As for the murder, expect the police to see you soon. By the way, I forgive you."

"I'm not taking this shit. Melissa is not leaving me. Let's go, wife." He was furious; I wasn't afraid of him anymore.

He became more enraged when Melissa didn't move. "Let's go, Melissa!"

"Don't yell at me. I will go to the car when I am ready. I am aware you not stupid enough to hit me in front of my people. Now, are you? You go to the damn car." She said in a disrespectful tone. She had enough of all his lies.

He did what she told him. He kissed her on the cheek and proceeded outside. I think he got a rise out of it, which made me nauseous.

Everybody became uneasy when she walked up to me. She grabbed and hugged me.

"Cousin. I'm sorry." She was whispering to me. Her eyes were full of tears under her shades. I could feel her sorrows on my shoulders. "We will be ok. I'm going to make this right. I love you." She released me. "Terrence, I'm sorry. I hope you can forgive me."

Terrence said nothing. She walked out the door, head hanging in shame. Once she was gone, Jay and I explained to the entire family how Jim murdered Jay's brother, Shamar. It was a lot to take inside. So together, we prayed and apologized to one another. It was amazing to see my Uncle John & my mother make amends. Everybody hung out more and was getting set to watch the Green Bay vs. Kansas City game.

"Mom, this is nice. But Jay and I are coming back. We will make the liquor run for the guys."

Dani and Terrence gave each other funny stares. They were cracking up in laughter, thinking of me picking up the drinks.

"Nephew, don't bring no fa-." Uncle John looked at my mother. "I mean no fruity drinks."

I let out a surprising cackle. "Unc, I'm bringing back Ciroc. I got this."

He winked at me. It was my first positive interaction with him since I was little.

So Jay and I left. We traveled to pick up the liquor. However, we took a detour to the lakefront.

13

DEADLY REPERCUSSIONS

W e drove up and parked where Shamar always led me. We sat down on one of the top steps. I enjoyed feeling the wind chill on this Sunday evening.

"So…" Jevaun said with an exhale, "I see why my brother comes out here. It's pretty nice."

"Yeah, It's pretty nice and calm. I can relax and think here."

"Hello, Aiden." I recognized that voice. We stood up.

"Hi, Angèle."

"Little Homie, who is this lady?" Jevaun asked me.

"She is someone who helped me."

Angèle gave me the Gros Bon Ange card. It is the Sun card in the New Orleans Voodoo Tarot.

"You will achieve happiness," she stated. She disappeared along with everybody else.

WE LOOKED at each other funny. It was like we were on the lakefront by ourselves. We looked around, seeing there was no one in sight.

Suddenly, there was a light that beamed from the heavens. The light had blinded us, a quick second meeting our feet. Jay and I quickly turned our heads. I smiled as Jay experienced his eyes swell up.

Shamar was walking towards in all white. "Hi, you two. Thank you. Everything will be ok. I can't touch you guys, but there is something I can do."

He made something like a wind swirl around us. It felt like he was giving us a friendly hug full of thanks and love.

"But, I am waiting for someone before I leave you."

"Aiden," a voice said in a whisper.

It was a voice recognized. It was Melissa.

"What are you doing here?" I said. It had puzzled me to see her. I realized her clothes were slowly turning white. I wanted to scream. It would not come out. "Wait. Not you. This can't be happening. I thought we had a real chance to start over."

She grabbed me in a hug, with Shamar rubbing my back. She showed us what happened.

MELISSA COULDN'T BELIEVE this was her life. Her cousin still blamed her for PawPaw's and Uncle Connor's accident. Then she wished Momo Jean and Aunt Joanne had told her exactly what Jim had done. She didn't hate her cousin. Her thoughts were he got a little more attention from everyone else.

She got in the car, and she closed the door. SMACK!

"Pick your glasses up. I can't wait to get you home. How the fuck you let that happen?! Your people. Embarrass me. Like that?!" Jim said in a roar.

She said nothing when she picked up her glasses. In her head, she was praying to God for forgiveness and her soul. If something happened between her and her husband, she knew it would be him or her. Her being scorned and reuniting with her family was her drive. She took her phone out.

Jacob. Meet me at my house now.

They pulled into their driveway, both of them got out, all cool and collected. But once inside, Jim went to hit her. He missed, but she dropped her phone. She hurried away into their bedroom and locked herself in their room. When Jim heard the lock, he decides he would go to the utility closet to retrieve his other weapon. When she got his 9 mm out of his end table, a letter flew out of it.

Jim knew she would find that letter he wrote about himself.

Melissa sat on her bed, tears streaming down her face as she read her husband's letter.

～

DEAR WHOEVER FINDS THIS,

I have done some horrible things in my past and present. I think I will find solace in the next life, hopefully. The cycle of abuse continued with me.

I never knew who my father was. Rebecca was a drug addict and alcoholic mother, who sold me and my sister, Camille, as sex slaves to Louis and Eunice Kingston. Louis trained me to be an "LD" lad. I helped him push drugs selling them to the community. He took it to a whole new level once he became the pastor of Saint Mark Baptist Church. He made me one of his head deacons all while I watched them raised the child I had with his wife—a little girl named Dinah, who called me her Uncle Jim.

I wasn't kicked out of the church until I "took advantage" of Aiden. I needed him to be an "LD" boy too. He didn't like the "initiation". I never looked back, leaving in 2009.

I wanted to become someone new in New Orleans. So I went to the doctor. It was something I never did in Marais Vert under

Louis's advice. I found out I was HIV positive. I got on medicine right away.

So I began a new life. The job of welding professor at NOLA Weld Tech opened doors for me. I didn't know I would like Melissa when I met her. Then I saw Little Nut. Her brother, Jacob. I was honest with both of them about my condition. Plus, finding out Aiden was her cousin. I could pick and torment him. All my demons started surfacing.

Dinah found out she was my daughter would come and visit me secretly. I begged her to stay. But tragedy struck Louis, Eunice, and Dinah in 2013.

Then in Shamar walks into my classroom. We carried on our affair until Jacob popped him for me. Shamar was going to tell everything. I knew I could trust Little Nut. He handled it. Damn. Even though I fell for him, something about Aiden made me tingle.

If someone is viewing it, my time is up either I'm going to kill myself or get killed. I hope God can forgive me. I can't run anymore.

Jim

P.S. If my wife is learning this, I'm not sorry for anything. Hurt people hurt people.

SHE WAS SO disgusted with him. Her fingers unlocked the door. The steps she took to the living room were slow and steady. That is where she met her husband. They had guns drawn on each other, pointing at each other's chests. Jim faced the door with his rifle.

"So you really did all this shit?" Melissa asked Jim in hysterical anger.

"You just wanted money. That's why you felt like you got what you deserve."

Just then, Jacob enters the house from the front door.

"No!!!" he said in a yell. He took out his gun.

POP! POP! Jacob shot his sister. She didn't even see it coming.

"Wait," Jim said. He put his gun on the floor. "Aww fuck. Little Nut, come help me move her."

Jacob rushed down to help her. Then he noticed the letter. He skimmed through it but read the last two paragraphs. His anger grew more. Jim was still kneeling down over his spouse with his back turned from Jacob.

"Am I better than Aiden?" Jacob asked.

"Man, what?" It puzzled Jim why he asked that question. Especially at a time like this. "No."

"No! Ok." Jacob pumped two bullets into Jim's back. He fell dead over his wife. Then Jacob pointed the gun under his chin and took his own life. Police arrived 5 minutes later and found all three people deceased in the home.

MELISSA'S CLOTHES were now completely white.

"I must go now. Cousin, it's ok. I have forgiven everyone," she said in a sweet tone.

I now wished I told her to stay at the house. Melissa disappeared from in front of me. She reappeared beside Shamar as Jay and I turned around.

"We will watch you from above. I think you will take comfort in that."

I looked towards the top of the light. My hands wiped my sad tears, and silent, happy tears replaced them. A sweet little lady I recognized was there. She wore her ushers' uniform as she stood at the entranceway of the light.

"Come on, children. We have been waiting for you," Momo Jean said sweetly. My grandmother looked at me and winked.

Jay and I blinked, and everything was back to normal on the lakefront. People were talking and riding their bikes. There was no sight of Shamar, Melissa, and Momo Jean. Suddenly, Jay's phone rang. Jay answered it as we ran back to the car. In the bushes, I heard another phone. I picked it up and brought it with me.

"That was Majo. She was calling to tell us to hurry back to the house. Aiden, are you ok?" Jay said in a sad tone. His voice turned from low to shocked. "Wait, is that Shamar's phone?"

"Yep. It is. We have to turn it into the police before we get it back. I'm not ok, but I will be."

I did not imagine life taking this route. All this started with a simple message on the HBG app. Jevaun turned "Moment 4 Life" on the radio as I gazed at him. While preparing myself to grieve, I prepared myself for my future with my prayers, family, dreams, and new best friend. Everything was looking up for me now. I truly appreciate having another chance for a positive outlook on life.

EPILOGUE

FEBRUARY 20, 2020

The night sky befell the levee. Jevaun and I were sitting out there. We made bottles of Big Blue mixed with Seagram's Blue Beast.

I thought of how life had changed since October. There were some positives. Jevaun started mending his relationship with his mom. My mom called her and pleaded with her to make amends. She also sent her links from The Trevor Project. He goes and visits his mom now and then.

We started a company together: We Jivin' Entertainment. I would take care of the online store, and Jevaun would control making music and signing artists to fair deals. We started working with an artist named Xavier Phlick. We believe in his talents and ideas. So this year is looking bright already.

I leaned my head against his shoulder, thinking of the bad. For me to go to 2 funerals was heart-breaking. No one blamed me for Jacob and Melissa's death. I still felt guilty; I didn't get a chance to make honorable amends with them.

"I bought you this, A.J. I hope you like it." Jay pulls out a golden dog tag with our business logo on it. He pulled the one he had out from underneath his shirt. "I already have mine."

"I guess we think a lot alike." I pulled out the rose gold watches with our logo on them. "We are in business together until the end of time, huh?"

We did our signature handshake. I was all smiles until Jay took his phone out. He started playing an R&B songstress I used to like.

"Cut that off, please. I don't listen to her anymore."

"Now, Little Homie, damn. What she did?"

I pulled up the articles and the screenshots of her HIV comments.

"You know, I canceled the other person. It's only fair that I stop supporting this artist, too. It doesn't matter how much I liked her music. Again, many blessings to her. I can't support anyone who does that."

"Well, let me take…"

POP!

"Get down now!" Jay said. There was so much fear and concern in his tone. We laid flat.

POP! POP!

I was lying down. I saw a figure running away from what they did. They left quickly, and we felt the coast was clear. She was at the bottom, near the water. We ran to the victim to help as I fumbled to dial 911.

"Hello, 911. I am on the levee. Someone shot this young lady. Please hurry."

I stayed on the phone with them. She was lying face up, struggling to breathe. She was the color of toffee, with a short buzz cut. There was blood all over her jeans and a golden t-shirt. Jevaun kept trying to assure her help was on the way. Tears came down her eyes. I was trying not to panic watching this young woman.

"Big Bat shot me." Then she took her last breath and died. The police arrive 5 minutes later. We came out here to chill. We could not have imagined witnessing a murder on the levee.

www.ingramcontent.com/pod-product-compliance
Lightning Source LLC
Chambersburg PA
CBHW071120100726

47908CB00008B/2437